When the Silence Speaks

Rene' Stanley

This is a work of fiction. Any resemblance to actual events or persons, living or dead, is purely coincidental. The story, all names, characters, and incidents portrayed in this production are fictitious. No identification with actual persons (living or deceased), places, buildings, and products is intended or should be inferred.

ISBN: 979-8-9997823-4-2 (paperback)

Cover Design by Rene' Stanley

Library of Congress Control Number: 2025922589

bbr@renes-books.us

https://booksbyrene.com

1 edition 2025

Contents

Breaking Ground

Samuel left the house at five-thirty, before Essie woke. Prayer before the day's noise was his discipline. The work demanded it, and the vacant lot on Jefferson Street was waiting.

The city was quiet except for a distant rail whistle and a dog's answering bark. Voices would come later, when the porches filled. Samuel walked the three blocks with his hands in his pockets, breathing the cool air. The lot smelled of turned earth and old cigarette ash. A stubborn patch of summer grass had survived the clearing.

He knelt where the foundation would be and pressed his palms into the dirt.

"Lord," he said, "help me not lose my temper when the measurements don't line up." The words came out quiet, mostly to himself. He did not ask for miracles. He asked for endurance—to stand when answers were late, to remain faithful when results lagged behind faithfulness.

When he rose, the sun was clearing the roofline of the houses across the street. He stood there a moment, studying the ground. This place would hold something permanent. People whose names he would never know would walk through that door someday, would kneel where he was kneeling now. He could not see them yet, but he felt the weight of their future presence.

The ground wanted a voice, and he had one.

He pulled the measuring tape from his pocket and got to work.

children slung on hips, with hymnals tucked under arms, with buckets of coffee and plates wrapped in cloth. Men came in rumpled suits and women in hats pinned high and proud. Laughter moved through the crowd—hard-earned, brittle, and hopeful. Some folks called out greetings. Others just nodded, their faces tired but lit with something close to joy. Ruth, still only a child with knees like soft furniture and braids that swung when she walked

and tried to keep up with the elders who stretched their memories beyond the hush of present fears.

Samuel stood now on the edge of a circle—his circle, ordained not by paper but by the way people leaned toward him when he spoke. He lifted his Bible, not because he needed to display it, but because the book felt, in his hands, like he was holding the building plans for a work he had not yet seen. He opened to Habakkuk and the verse he had kept in his mouth the past season. He did not read it to them as a sermon yet; he let it sit like a stone in the small pool of the moment and then he reached for it: "Write the vision, and make it plain on tablets, that he may run who reads it."

"Write the vision," he said aloud. "Tell it plain enough that a child can run with it. That's what we're doing here." His voice was even, the bass of it steady like a metronome. "This church won't be marble. It won't come with brass rails and white columns. It'll be a place where children learn and where old folks can sleep their prayers. Mount Zion will be a shelter in the storms. Amen?"

"Amen!" the people answered, and the sound folded up into the sky.

He could sense doubts in the faces: the slightly crooked mouths, the hands that rubbed at the dirt on their knees as if cleaning away doubt as if it were a stain. Essie stood beside him—a figure that had always, in Samuel's life, smoothed the furrows where storms had cut him. Her hands, set with age and household wisdom, were busy arranging the women who had come to bake, to sew, to fold. She did not look up immediately at his words. Instead, she measured the sky and the horizon and then, finally, looked at him with a patience that had kept him from collapsing into despair more times than he could count.

"Samuel," she said softly, not to refute the vision but to temper it with the ledger books of reality. "You talk of tablets and running. Who's paying for the bricks? Who's making sure the stones don't fall on the children when a storm comes?"

He knew the question would come. They had argued over this before—after the meeting at the parsonage when the bills lay like small dead fishes on the table. His answer was never monetary at first. Faith was not a contract; it was a stubborn insistence that work had worth beyond its account balance. "We will find the money," he said. "Lord provides in ways we do not expect. We do what we can with what we have. The scripture is plain: we write the vision."

Essie's eyes found his and a smile, half wry and half pleading, curved the corner of her mouth. She moved closer and placed a hand on his cheek. "I've seen 'Lord provides' before. I've seen men promise the moon and bring us sugar for the bread. Promise me you won't gamble with the children's meals."

"Never," he promised, and he meant it.

Ruth drifted away from them and wandered the perimeter of the lot with the easy curiosity of someone collecting seeds. She paused by an old slab of concrete where moss grew like slow green handwriting and listened to a group of elders who sat on overturned crates. The oldest among them—Mother Caldwell, with hair the color of bone and a voice that had survived more winters than the lot had seen summers—was telling the story of the church before the church: of house meetings on back porches, of clandestine hymnals hidden under flour sacks.

"You don't forget how to pray," Mother Caldwell said, her voice rasping like dry leaves. " It keeps the meat from going bad."

Ruth sat on the concrete and heard the cadence of the women's words. The story seeped into her as if it were honey into bread: this place had always been for holding, for keeping. She picked up a pebble and traced the edge of it with her thumb. Somewhere close a choir began to hum, the notes wrinkling the air like heat. She rehearsed the shape of a spiritual tune under her breath until the melody felt like a secret she owned.

Not all voices at the lot were friendly. At midmorning a black truck rolled up slowly and stopped at the edge of the gathering. Samuel saw it, the way a preacher sees a ripple cross the congregation. A tall man in a pale shirt got out, his hat in his hands—not the uniform of a sheriff, but the coolness of an official, a clipboard tucked under his arm as if he had the authority of a building inspector or a taxman. His smile did not reach his eyes.

"Good morning, Pastor," he said, and his voice was the softest kind of trouble. "Heard you're building here. County ordinance says you need a permit for anything that resembles a public assembly structure."

Samuel looked at him, at the clipboard, at the measured way the man's shoes had been cleaned. He felt every careful look like a weighing scale. "We're building a house of worship, sir," he said. "We'll follow the law."

"We wouldn't want anyone getting hurt," the man said, then added, as if relaying a kindness, "You understand how folks react when things change."

It was not a threat wrapped in threats, only the faintest whisper of a warning—keep your place. The language of the lot, too, had its own proprietors; in this county one held hands with danger by mistake. Samuel smiled with his mouth, but his heart tightened.

He could taste the old bitterness he had tasted in Memphis as a boy, the rawness of a world that kept doors closed.

"Sir," he said, the word a prayer and a warning both, "we'll build no lawless thing. But we won't let fear tell us where to kneel."

The man's smile thinned, like a note cut from the chorus. He tucked his clipboard tighter to his chest and, without another word, turned and started back toward his truck. The engine coughed to life and the vehicle rolled away, leaving a faint cloud of dust that settled over the lot—like a thin veil that could be lifted.

Afterward, silence collected in the corners of the circle. The children picked at the dust with their fingers, making small mounds of future hills. Someone began a hymn with a single note, and the congregation took it up like a tide. Samuel walked to the center of the lot where the first brick would be placed. He could have postponed the moment—he had reasons to postpone, to let paperwork and permits find their way in fluorescent-lit rooms. But faith, for him, was not a leash for common sense; it was the impulse to act when action and prayer met in the same hand.

He took the trowel with the same attention he gave to the Bible in his hands. It felt right in his palm—wood worn smooth by earnest labor. A man with broad shoulders and a face like a promise set down the mortar. Women passed bowls of water and rags. Ruth stood close enough to see the lines on Samuel's hands, the veins that carried more than blood: they carried the history of those who bent to make holy things.

He placed the first brick slowly, as if laying down a favorite name.

The congregation hummed low, their voices threading together until the sound wrapped around everyone present like shared breath.

Essie stood by, her apron tied more like an armor than clothing. Later she would chide him for not having weighed the costs, but now she let the stone settle, let the dust fall into the right grooves. A child nearby clapped because something important had happened—maybe because adults were being serious in a way that made them seem ancient and true.

Samuel took a step back and looked at the brick as if he were seeing the face of a child for the first time. It fit into the circle of other hands and plans and prayers. The sun, which had been thin and tentative, nudged itself higher and sent a single shaft through the shoulders of a sycamore tree. The light fell clean across the brick and made it almost sing, as if stained glass had opened up in the sky.

Someone began to sing with a little more courage now—a spiritual about waiting and about the Lord who both asks for patience and honors labor. The voices rose, braided and strong. Samuel closed his eyes and let the song hold him. It was not a triumph; it was the sound of people who had been told they should not build and decided, by the grace of a stubborn calling, to build anyway.

Essie slid her hand into his. "You keep us honest, Samuel Washington," she said.

"You keep us fed," he replied, and they both laughed a small, dry laugh that carried the relief of townsfolk who had survived another night.

When they worked again, the men laid brick; the women swept; the children ran in circles and carried pebbles like blessings. The day went on the way a prayer that keeps answering itself goes on—longer than hope, shorter than fear. Samuel watched faces as much as he watched the wall rise. He watched the way young men's shoulders straightened when they had a place to set their strength against. He watched old women sip tea and dream and say Amen with the particular conviction of those who had little left to lose.

By afternoon the first course of bricks sat true. The foundation had its first voice. Samuel ran his hand along the mortar, feeling the rough softness of it—the grain that would eventually smooth with time and hands, like the backs of so many necks. In his pocket his Bible seemed lighter, as if joy could be stored in leather and clap like coins. He looked up and the sun slid through a cloud and struck the lot in a way that made dust drop like a slow rain. Light pooled in places where shadows had been long. It was as if something older than fear had come to stand with them.

When the day cooled and folks started to file away toward homes that smelled of broth and soap, Samuel stood for a moment more on the newly made edge and let the quiet roll over him. He was not naive. He knew the county inspector could come back and he knew men who liked the quiet ways the world remained unfair. He knew that waiting could turn a man bitter if he let it. But he also knew that faith arranged time itself—faith could make the slow a kind of answer.

Ruth ran up, breathless, her shoes smudged with the same dust that clung to the mortar. She put both small hands on the first brick and looked up at Samuel with eyes that already believed him the way children believe saints.

"Do you think it will stand, Pastor?" she asked.

"It will stand," he said, and he let the words be an offering and a prophecy both. Behind him Essie and the congregation were slipping back into their homes, into the ordinary labor of living. The lot, for all the work yet undone, held the light like a promise.

Samuel watched the sun slip toward late afternoon and thought, not boastfully but with hard gratitude, of the tablets he hoped to write. Write the vision and make it plain, he thought again. Let it be plain enough to run. Let it be plain enough that even the children could see and know when to lift their feet.

A breeze moved through the sycamore and carried with it the sound of voices folding into music, a hymn that would ring in the place long after the mortars dried.

Ruth stepped forward and placed both hands on the brick, her palms flat against the cool clay. "Do you think it will stand?"

Samuel looked at the brick, then at her hands, then at the empty lot that would become Mount Zion.

"It will stand."

Seeds in Hard Ground

The hammer found its rhythm in the purple hour before dawn—three strikes, pause, three strikes. Samuel's hands moved with the economy of a man who had learned to make every motion count. The church frame rose board by board, but the work came slow. By day he taught school in a building that leaked when it rained and sweltered when it didn't. By night he built Mount Zion with hands that ached from sunrise to moonrise.

The sawhorses balanced on cinder blocks. The lumber—what little they could afford—lay stacked in the moonlight, twenty-three boards and counting. Samuel worked by the light of a kerosene lantern that threw his shadow long across the lot. His shirt clung to his back despite the cool air. Sweat was honest work, the price he paid with his body when money ran thin.

He paused to wipe his face with a handkerchief Essie had pressed into his pocket that morning. The cloth still held the faint scent of her hands—soap and flour and the particular sweetness of a woman who had learned to make much from little. Through the kitchen window of their house across the street, he could see the amber glow of her reading lamp. She would be bent over her ledger books, penciling numbers that never quite added up to enough, planning the impossible mathematics of faith.

Three more nails. The sound carried in the still air like a bell tolling the hour. Samuel set down the hammer and flexed his fingers. In the distance, a train whistle mourned its way toward

Charlotte, carrying freight and the dreams of folks who could afford tickets to somewhere else. He had been offered such a ticket once—a position at a church in Philadelphia, a salary that would have bought meat every Sunday and shoes that didn't let in the rain. He had turned it down because some calls were not about comfort but about staying, about putting down roots in ground that others had deemed too hard for growing.

The frame looked pitiful in the lantern light—a skeleton without flesh, a promise without proof. But Samuel had seen too many small miracles to trust only his eyes. The boy who had been born to sharecroppers in a cabin with newspaper for wallpaper had learned that God's arithmetic operated by different rules. What looked impossible at midnight often seemed merely difficult by morning.

He knelt by the foundation stones and ran his hand along the mortar they had laid the week before. It had set true and level. The first course of bricks waited under a tarp, patient as sleeping children. Tomorrow the men would come after their own work was done—James from the rail yard, Moses from the cotton warehouse, young David who swept floors at the bank and sang bass in their little choir. They would bring their own tiredness and their own small hopes, and together they would raise another course.

Samuel picked up his hammer again. Three strikes, pause, three strikes. The rhythm was a kind of prayer, a conversation between his hands and the wood, between his will and the morning that would surely come.

By mid-morning the lot bustled with the particular energy of women on a mission. Essie had arrived at sunrise with a delegation of church mothers, their arms full of quilting squares and ambitious plans. They had taken over the shade of the old oak tree, transforming it into a command center for what she called "the Lord's fundraising campaign." Ruth sat cross-legged in the dirt nearby, folding squares of colored paper into the pockets of seed packets—each one containing information about the church building fund along with actual seeds for late-season greens.

"Every garden tells a story about patience," Essie explained to the circle of women who cut and folded with the practiced efficiency of those who had made miracles from scraps their entire lives. "These folks plant our seeds, they'll remember Mount Zion every time they see those turnip greens come up."

Mother Caldwell nodded from her chair, her ancient hands surprisingly nimble with the needle. "Smartest thing I heard all week. Can't nobody eat a sermon, but they sure can eat what grows from it."

Ruth looked up from her folding. "Mama, what if the seeds don't grow?"

"Then we plant more," Essie replied without hesitation. "Some ground takes more working than other ground. But everything wants to grow, baby girl. Just got to find the right season for it."

Ruth had volunteered to deliver the seed packets to the neighborhoods beyond their immediate circle—the streets where porches sagged under the weight of too many hopes deferred, where children played in yards that dust had claimed and poverty had hardened. She walked with the particular awareness of a child who had learned to read the temperature of a place through the eyes of the adults who watched her pass.

On Elm Street, she knocked on the door of a shotgun house where Mrs. Patterson lived with her three grandchildren. The woman who answered had the kind of tired that sleep couldn't cure, but her face softened when she saw Ruth's small hands holding the packet.

"From Mount Zion Baptist," Ruth said, repeating the words Essie had coached her to say. "We're building a church for the whole community. These are turnip green seeds, and there's information about how you can help if the Lord moves your heart."

Mrs. Patterson took the packet and turned it over in her palm. "Your daddy's the preacher, ain't he? The one building over on the lot by himself?"

"Yes ma'am. But he's not by himself. We all helping."

"I heard tell he's got big dreams for a little church."

Ruth straightened her shoulders the way she had seen her mother do when faced with doubt disguised as kindness. "Daddy says dreams got to start somewhere. And small don't mean not important."

Mrs. Patterson smiled then, a real smile that reached her eyes. "You tell your daddy I said that's a wise child he's raising. And I'll plant these seeds. See what the Lord has in mind for my little patch of dirt."

Ruth walked home with her small chest swelled with pride, but the feeling dimmed as she turned onto Broad Street. A group of white boys, older than her and dressed in clothes that spoke of allowances and parents who drove new cars, blocked the sidewalk ahead. They had the particular stillness of predators who had found something to toy with.

"Look here," one called out as she approached. "Little church girl making house calls."

Ruth's hand tightened on the remaining seed packets. She had been taught to look adults in the eye when speaking, but these weren't adults, and her mama's lessons about respect warred with her daddy's teachings about not letting folks diminish your light.

"Excuse me," she said quietly, trying to step around them.

"What you selling, girl? Magic beans?" The tallest boy snatched one of the packets from her hand and tore it open, letting the seeds scatter across the pavement like dark tears. "Look like regular old seeds to me. Nothing magic about 'em."

Ruth watched the seeds fall and felt something hot and sharp rise in her chest. Those seeds represented hours of the church mothers' work, pennies scraped together from grocery money, hope packaged in paper and prayer. But more than that, they represented her daddy's dream taking root in other people's hands, and now they lay trampled under the shoes of boys who would never understand what it meant to build something from nothing.

"They're not magic," she said, her voice stronger than she felt. "They're just seeds. But they'll grow into something that feeds people. And that's better than magic."

The boys laughed, but something in Ruth's steady gaze made the laughter sound forced. She bent down and began gathering the scattered seeds, her small hands working with deliberate care. She couldn't save them all—some had already been ground into the concrete—but she saved what she could. When she stood up, the boys had lost interest and wandered away, their attention caught by some other cruelty.

Ruth walked the rest of the way home with dirt under her fingernails and tears she refused to let fall burning behind her eyes. She had learned something important about the distance between planting and harvesting, about the things that could be lost between intention and growth. But she had also learned that some seeds were worth gathering even when they seemed ruined, that the act of caring for broken things was its own kind of faithfulness.

The evening brought Samuel's favorite part of the day—the time when folks came by the lot not to work but to sit and talk while the air cooled and children played between the lumber piles. James had brought his guitar, and Moses contributed a harmonica that caught the light like silver water when he played. The men sat on upturned crates and nail kegs, their work clothes dusty with the day's labor, their voices weaving together stories that were part complaint, part testimony, and part dream.

But tonight the conversation carried an undercurrent that made Samuel's chest tight. Word had come from over in Greenwood County—another lynching. A young man named Thomas, barely twenty, accused of looking too long at a white woman outside the five-and-dime. The details were whispered rather than spoken aloud, but they settled over the group like smoke from a fire that wouldn't quite go out.

"Makes a man wonder," Moses said, his harmonica quiet in his lap, "what we building this church for if the world still got that kind of hate in it."

Samuel looked around the circle of faces—good men who worked honest jobs and loved their families and deserved to live without fear. He felt the weight of their expectation, the burden of being the one who was supposed to have answers when questions cut too deep for easy comfort.

And here's what I keep coming back to: we building this church because the world has that kind of hate in it. The hate itself is the reason. We're answering it with something stronger.

He stood and walked to the frame they had raised, placing his hand on one of the support beams. "This here wood ain't going to stop hatred. But it's going to hold up a roof. And under that roof, we going to raise children who know their worth don't come from what other folks think of them. We going to sing songs that remind us who we are when the world tries to tell us who we ain't."

James strummed a quiet chord, a sound that seemed to echo in the growing darkness. "Pastor, you really think singing and praying going to change men's hearts?"

Samuel turned to face them, these men who trusted him with their doubts and their desperate need for hope. "I think singing and praying changes our hearts. And changed hearts do different work in the world. Thomas—God rest his soul—he deserved better than what they gave him. But if we let fear stop us from building, if we let hatred convince us to hide, then we letting them kill more than one young man. We letting them kill the future."

A long silence settled over the group. In the distance, a whip-poorwill called from the woods beyond the railroad tracks. Ruth emerged from the house across the street, drawn by the sound of voices and the soft glow of James's cigarette ember. She settled herself on the steps where she could listen without being noticed, the way children do when they sense that important words are being spoken.

"Tell you what's true," Mother Caldwell's voice rose from her chair in the shadows. They hadn't seen her arrive, but she had a way of appearing when wisdom was needed most. "I been alive long enough to see hatred dressed up in all kinds of clothes. Sometimes it wear a sheet, sometimes it wear a badge, sometimes it wear a smile and offer you a job you know you ain't going to get."

She rocked forward slightly, her chair creaking like old floor-boards. "Love comes dressed up in all kinds of ways too. Love that builds schools and love that hides runaway children and love that stands up in court even when standing up means falling down. This church we building? It's love wearing the clothes of wood and nails. And that's the kind of love that outlasts hate, because love knows how to wait."

Samuel felt something loosen in his chest, a knot of fear and responsibility that had been tightening all day. Mother Caldwell had lived through Reconstruction and the false promises that followed, through decades of small hopes and smaller victories. If she could still speak of love outlasting hate, if she could still believe in the value of building when destruction seemed to have all the power, then maybe his faith wasn't naive. Maybe it was simply well-informed.

"Mother Caldwell," he said, "you always know just what we need to hear."

"Honey," she replied with a chuckle that carried the sound of rain on a tin roof, "I been practicing these speeches for seventy years. About time they started making sense."

The laughter that followed was soft and real, the kind that happens when people realize they are not alone with their fears. James picked up his guitar again and began the opening notes of "Precious Lord," and one by one the voices joined in. Ruth listened from the steps as the song rose and fell, carried on air that still held the day's heat and the promise of tomorrow's work.

When the last note faded, the men began to pack up their instruments and gather their things. The workday would start early, and Mount Zion would wait for them as she had been waiting—patient as turned earth, stubborn as faith itself.

Samuel walked to the foundation one more time before heading home. In the darkness, he could barely make out the outline of what they were building, but he could feel its presence like a prayer taking shape. Tomorrow there would be more lumber to cut, more nails to drive, more reasons to doubt and more reasons to continue. Tonight, though, in the space between Mother Caldwell's wisdom and the sound of men's voices joined in song, he felt something he hadn't felt in weeks: the quiet certainty that they were not building alone.

The interruption came at dawn on Thursday, when Samuel was measuring lumber for the window frames. A soft knock at the front door pulled Essie from her kitchen, and Ruth heard the murmur of women's voices followed by her mother's sharp intake of breath. Samuel looked up from his work to see Essie hurrying across the lot, her apron still tied around her waist and her face carrying the particular tight expression that meant news had arrived faster than anyone was ready for it.

"Samuel," she called, not loudly but with an urgency that made him set down his tools immediately. "Mrs. Henderson's here. Says there's a family needs help."

Mrs. Henderson was a small woman who cleaned houses on the north side of town, moving through white neighborhoods with the near-invisibility that domestic work required. She was also part of a network that Samuel knew existed but rarely spoke about directly—a chain of communication that stretched through kitchen doors and back alleys, carrying information that never appeared in newspapers.

"Pastor Washington," she said when he reached the house, her voice barely above a whisper despite the fact that they stood in his own front room. "There's a family hiding in my basement. Been there two days. They need to get north, but the sheriff's got men watching the main roads."

Samuel felt his pulse quicken. He had heard the stories—sharecroppers who tried to leave before their debts were marked paid, families who disappeared in the night rather than face another season of hopelessness disguised as legal contracts. The Underground Railroad had officially ended decades ago, but its spirit lived on in the quiet courage of people who understood that sometimes salvation required breaking unjust laws.

"How many?" he asked.

"Four. Mama, daddy, two little ones. The daddy tried to leave Pearson's farm last week. Said he'd worked off what he owed, but Pearson's got different mathematics. They came looking for him yesterday with dogs and ropes."

Samuel looked at Essie, whose face had gone pale but whose jaw was set with the determination he had fallen in love with twenty years ago. They both knew what helping meant—the immediate danger, yes, and also the long-term risk to their own family, to the church, to everything they were trying to build.

"Where do they need to go?" Essie asked, because she had already made the decision and was moving on to logistics.

"Got family in Norfolk. Railroad job waiting if he can get there."

Samuel walked to the window and looked out at the lot where Mount Zion waited, her frame naked against the morning sky. The church was supposed to be a sanctuary, but it was still weeks from having walls, months from having doors that could close and lock. Yet sanctuary lived in people willing to risk something precious for someone else's freedom. The idea had always been about hearts more than buildings.

"Bring them tonight," he said. "After midnight. We'll get them to the next station."

Mrs. Henderson nodded and slipped out the back door, moving with the practiced invisibility that had kept her safe and useful for so many years. Samuel and Essie stood in their front room, looking at each other with the weight of what they had just committed to settling between them like dust.

"You sure about this?" Essie asked, though her tone suggested she would support whatever choice he made.

"I'm sure we can't build a house of God on a foundation of turning away from God's children when they need help," Samuel replied. "I'm also sure it's dangerous. For us, for Ruth, for everyone who comes to that lot on Sunday mornings."

"Then we be extra careful and extra prayerful," Essie said with the matter-of-fact tone she used for all problems that required more faith than sense. "And we trust the Lord to cover what we can't cover ourselves."

That night Ruth was sent to bed early with instructions to stay there no matter what sounds she heard. She lay in the dark listening to her parents move through the house with deliberate quiet—the soft thump of supplies being gathered, the whispered conversation that carried the weight of serious plans. Through her window she could see the church frame silhouetted against the stars, and she wondered if the building itself could feel the danger that seemed to hover over the lot like storm clouds.

At twelve-thirty, shadows moved across the backyard. Samuel had positioned himself at the kitchen window where he could see the approaches to the house. Essie waited by the cellar door with a basket of food and clean clothes. The family arrived like ghosts—four figures moving in single file, the parents carrying children who had learned to be silent when silence meant survival.

Samuel opened the door before they could knock. The man was young, maybe twenty-five, with the kind of lean strength that came from field work and the haunted eyes of someone who had seen too much violence disguised as law. The woman carried a baby who couldn't have been more than two, while a boy of perhaps five clung to her skirt with the desperate grip of a child who understood that losing hold meant losing everything.

"You're safe here," Samuel whispered as he ushered them inside. "But we can't stay long."

The man tried to speak, to offer thanks or explanation, but Samuel shook his head. "Save your words for when you're free to speak them loud," he said. "Right now we just need to get you to tomorrow."

They moved through the night like a prayer made visible. Samuel drove his old truck with the family hidden under canvas in the back, following back roads that wound through pine forests and tobacco fields. Essie stayed home to maintain the appearance of normalcy, but Samuel knew she would not sleep until he returned. The truck's engine sounded unnaturally loud in the darkness, and every pair of headlights in the rearview mirror made his hands tighten on the steering wheel.

The next station was a farmhouse fifteen miles north, owned by a Quaker family whose ancestors had been hiding runaway slaves since before the Civil War. Samuel had met them only once before, but when he knocked on their door at two in the morning, they opened it without question and welcomed the family with the practiced efficiency of people who had been doing this work for generations.

"They'll be in Norfolk by Sunday," the farmer assured Samuel as they transferred the small bundles of belongings from truck to wagon. "Got a job lined up at the shipyard and a place to stay until they can get on their feet."

Samuel shook the man's hand and felt the calluses that spoke of honest labor, the firm grip that spoke of shared commitment to something larger than themselves. He thought of the words from Exodus that had been running through his mind all night: "You shall not oppress a stranger, for you know the heart of a stranger, because you were strangers in the land of Egypt."

The drive home passed without incident, but Samuel's heart didn't resume its normal rhythm until he saw the familiar outline of Mount Zion's frame against the predawn sky. The church looked exactly as he had left it—unfinished, vulnerable, hopeful. Something had shifted, though, in his understanding of what they were building. Sunday worship and Wednesday prayer meeting would fill this space eventually, yes. And so would the work of love that required risk. Sanctuary in the truest sense—a place where God's children could find refuge when the world turned hard against them.

Essie met him at the door with coffee and the particular smile she reserved for moments when she was proud of them both. "How do you feel?" she asked.

Samuel thought about it as he sipped the coffee that tasted like normal life resuming after extraordinary circumstances. "Like we laid another course of bricks tonight," he said finally. "The invisible kind that hold everything else up."

Outside the window, the church frame waited for another day's work. But Samuel understood now that the real building had been happening all along, in moments like this when people chose love over fear, service over safety, faith over the easy mathematics of self-preservation– the risks taken for strangers, the quiet insistence that sanctuary meant more than shelter, the stubborn refusal to let hatred have the last word. Mount Zion was rising from lumber and nails, yes, and also from the decisions made in midnight kitchens, from the courage of people who opened doors when opening meant danger, from the conviction that God's house started with God's work wherever that work needed doing.

Sunday morning brought the kind of heat that made the air shimmer like water and turned work clothes into second skins. The congregation gathered in the shade of the oak tree, their folding chairs arranged in loose rows that faced the unfinished church frame. Samuel had draped canvas between the support beams to create a makeshift wall, but the structure still looked more like promise than protection. He didn't mind. Some of his best preaching had been done under open sky, where the ceiling was high enough for prayers to reach heaven without impediment.

Ruth sat in the front row between Essie and Mother Caldwell, her small hands folded in her lap and her attention drifting between her father's words and the interesting pattern of shadows that moved across the ground as the sun climbed higher. She was still young enough to find sermons mysterious—not boring exactly, but full of words that seemed to mean more than they said and stories that felt important in ways she couldn't quite grasp.

Samuel stood before his congregation with his Bible open to Habakkuk, the same passage that had become his companion through the long nights of building and the longer nights of waiting for results that seemed perpetually just out of reach. He had preached on patience before, but today the words carried a different weight, seasoned by recent experience and the growing understanding that waiting was not passive but active, not resignation but resistance.

"The prophet says, 'Write the vision and make it plain on tablets, that he may run who reads it,'" Samuel began, his voice carrying easily in the still air. "But then he says something that stops folks in their tracks: 'For the vision is yet for an appointed time, but at the end it will speak, and it will not lie. Though it tarries, wait for it; because it will surely come, it will not tarry.'"

He paused to let the apparent contradiction settle in the minds of his listeners. Around the circle, faces reflected the particular attention that came when scripture touched the raw places where hope and experience rubbed against each other.

"Now that sounds like riddle talk, don't it? The vision won't tarry, but we got to wait for it? It will surely come, but we don't know when? Prophet's got some explaining to do."

A few amens rippled through the congregation, along with the kind of soft laughter that meant people recognized their own confusion reflected in the preacher's words.

"But see, the prophet understood something about time that we forget when we get caught up in wanting our prayers answered on our schedule. He understood that there's God's time and there's our time, and they don't always run on the same clock."

Samuel walked closer to the congregation, leaving his notes behind and speaking from the place where preparation met inspiration. "We been building this church for months now. Some of y'all getting tired hands. Some getting worried hearts. Some starting to wonder if maybe we bit off more than we can chew."

He could see heads nodding, the honest acknowledgment of doubts that had been whispered in kitchen conversations and carried like small burdens through sleepless nights.

"But I want to tell you something about this waiting we been doing. It ain't empty time. It ain't wasted time. While we been waiting, we been learning. Learning how to work together when the work gets hard. Learning how to share what little we got when sharing don't make sense. Learning how to hold onto hope when hope feels foolish."

Ruth straightened in her chair, remembering the seeds scattered on the pavement and the way she had gathered them despite their apparent ruin. Something in her father's words connected to that moment, to the decision to save what could be saved even when saving seemed pointless.

"Last week," Samuel continued, "I had occasion to help some folks who were in a difficult situation. Can't say much about the particulars, but I can say this: when the time came to choose between what was safe and what was right, this congregation chose right. And that choice, that willingness to risk something precious for someone else's freedom, that's not separate from building this church. That's part of building this church."

The congregation stirred with the recognition that comes when a preacher touches on something they have all been thinking about but haven't quite known how to name. The network of whispers that had carried news of the midnight rescue had also carried questions about whether they were putting their own dreams at risk for strangers' needs.

"See, we not just building a building," Samuel said, his voice rising with conviction. "We building a sanctuary. And a sanctuary ain't about walls that keep danger out. A sanctuary is about hearts that let love in. A sanctuary is about people who understand that their own freedom ain't complete until everybody's freedom is complete."

Mother Caldwell's voice rose from her chair like smoke from an altar: "Preach it, Pastor. Tell the truth."

"The vision Habakkuk wrote about—it's bigger than our little church. It's bigger than our little town. It's about a world where justice rolls down like water and righteousness like a mighty stream. And that vision, that dream, it's worth waiting for. It's worth working for. It's worth risking for."

Samuel's voice softened, becoming intimate rather than oratorical. "But while we waiting for that big vision to come to pass, we got small visions happening every day. Every time we choose love over fear, every time we share instead of hoard, every time we build instead of tear down—that's the vision speaking. That's the appointed time arriving right here, right now, in this moment."

He gestured toward the unfinished frame of Mount Zion, its raw lumber gleaming in the morning sun. "This church is going to stand, beloved. Maybe not as fast as we want, maybe not as fancy as we dream, but it's going to stand. Because it's built on more than concrete and timber. It's built on the faith of people who understand that waiting is not doing nothing—waiting is doing everything you can while you trust God to do everything you can't."

The congregation rose as one, not because anyone had called them to stand but because the words had lifted them beyond sitting. James reached for his guitar and Mother Caldwell began the opening line of "We Shall Overcome," her voice thin but true. One by one the other voices joined, creating harmony from individual hopes, strength from shared commitment.

Ruth sang along, not understanding all the words but feeling their power in her chest, their promise in her throat. She looked at the church frame and saw it differently now—not as an unfinished building but as a prayer taking shape, a vision learning how to speak. The canvas walls fluttered in the breeze like flags of surrender, but she understood now that surrender and resistance could be the same thing, that waiting and working were not opposites but partners in the slow dance of faith.

When the song ended, the congregation remained standing for a long moment, as if reluctant to break the spell of unity that had settled over them like morning dew. Finally, Samuel offered the benediction, his words carrying the weight of blessing and the lightness of hope: "May the Lord watch between me and thee while we are absent one from another. And may the work of our hands be established, in God's time and in God's way."

The timber felt solid under her palm, stubborn as the love that would finish it. Somewhere in the distance, a train whistle called out its lonesome song, carrying freight and dreams toward destinations unknown. But Ruth wasn't listening to the whistle. She was listening to the silence that lived inside the frame, the quiet space where prayers would soon be spoken and songs would soon be sung, where the vision would finally learn how to speak loud enough for the whole world to hear.

Small Mercies

Samuel's coffee had gone cold while he stood at the kitchen window. He'd been watching the half-finished walls of Mount Zion emerge from the morning fog for the better part of twenty minutes, mentally calculating what three more months of work might cost against what the building fund actually held.

October mist still clung to the church frame in patches. The structure stood shoulder-high now—three months of steady work visible in every course of brick—but autumn had brought more than cool mornings. It had brought the grinding reality of bills that came due whether the congregation's enthusiasm held or not. And lately, that enthusiasm had begun to meet its limits.

Behind him, Essie moved through the kitchen with practiced efficiency, the kind a woman develops after years of stretching coffee beans and making miracles from leftovers. The aroma of chicory filled the small room, mixing with the sound of her humming.

—a low, thoughtful melody that seemed to be working out problems too complex for words.

"Coffee's ready," she said, not because he had asked but because she understood the ritual that began each day: strong coffee, silent prayer, and the careful inventory of what needed doing versus what could actually be done. She poured two cups from the blue enamel pot that had been a wedding gift from her mother, a woman who had known how to make beauty from cast-offs and hope from scraps.

Samuel turned from the window and accepted the cup with hands that bore the honest scars of construction work—splinters healed over, calluses earned from hammer handles, the particular roughness that came from wrestling lumber into submission. "Building's starting to look like something," he said, though they both knew it was still months from resembling the vision he had cast that first morning on the lot.

"Mmm-hmm," Essie agreed, settling into her chair at the table where her ledger books lay open like prayer requests written in columns of figures. "Looking like something that needs a roof before winter sets in proper."

The mathematics were unforgiving. Samuel had spent the previous evening calculating and recalculating, trying to make their modest building fund stretch to cover roofing materials. The numbers stubbornly refused to cooperate, no matter how many times he rearranged them on paper. They had enough for half a roof, which was the same as having no roof at all when the Carolina rains came calling.

"Women's auxiliary made forty-three dollars at the bake sale," Essie continued, running her finger down a column of careful entries. "Mother Caldwell's pound cake alone brought in eight. That woman's got a gift that transcends cooking."

Samuel smiled despite his worries. Mother Caldwell's pound cake had become legendary in three counties, dense as a prayer and sweet as grace. Folks drove from as far away as Raleigh when they heard she was baking for Mount Zion, and her kitchen had become an unofficial headquarters for what she called "the Lord's fundraising campaign."

"Every little bit helps," Samuel said, settling into his own chair and opening his worn Bible to Habakkuk. The pages fell open automatically to chapter two, the verses worn soft from months of reading and rereading. "'For the vision is yet for an appointed time, but at the end it will speak, and it will not lie. Though it tarries, wait for it; because it will surely come, it will not tarry.'"

Essie looked up from her ledger. "You been living in that passage so long, I'm surprised the words haven't wore off the page."

"Some words bear repeating," Samuel replied. "Especially when the waiting gets longer than the hoping."

A soft knock at the back door interrupted their morning routine. Through the screen, they could see Mrs. Patterson from Elm Street, the same woman Ruth had visited with seed packets months earlier. She held a covered dish in her hands and wore the particular expression of someone who had wrestled with a decision all night and finally reached a conclusion.

"Morning, Pastor Washington. Mrs. Washington." She shifted the dish to one hand and smoothed her apron with the other. "I hope I'm not disturbing your breakfast."

"Never a disturbance," Essie said, rising to unlatch the screen door. "Come in and have some coffee. Pot's still warm."

Mrs. Patterson stepped into the kitchen, bringing with her the scent of fresh cornbread and the particular dignity of a woman who had learned to carry herself with grace despite circumstances that would have bent lesser spirits. She had raised three grandchildren on a cleaning woman's wages, kept them in school when the costs seemed impossible, and maintained a garden that fed half the neighborhood when times got especially hard.

"I brought cornbread," she said, setting the covered dish on the table. "Made extra this morning and thought maybe you folks could use it." She paused, then reached into her apron pocket and withdrew a small envelope. "And I wanted to give you this for the church building fund."

Samuel accepted the envelope with the careful attention he gave to all offerings, understanding that each contribution represented sacrifice measured not in dollars but in dreams deferred, meals simplified, small comforts foregone. The envelope was thin—perhaps a few bills folded with the reverence reserved for sacred things.

"Mrs. Patterson, you don't have to—"

"Pastor," she interrupted gently but firmly, "my grandchildren been eating greens from those seeds your little girl brought me. Every time we sit down to supper and see them turnips on the table, we remember that somebody planted hope in our yard. This is just hope returning the favor."

Essie reached across the table and covered Mrs. Patterson's weathered hand with her own. "That's the Lord's mathematics right there. Plant seeds, harvest blessings. Sometimes the harvest comes in ways we never expected."

After Mrs. Patterson left, Samuel opened the envelope to find three one-dollar bills and a handful of coins—perhaps four dollars in total, which would have represented a significant portion of a cleaning woman's weekly wages. But more than the money was the note written on a scrap of brown paper in the careful script of someone who had learned to write by lamplight after long days of labor:

For Mount Zion Baptist Church. These greens growing in my yard remind me every day that small seeds can become big blessings. Use this where it's needed most. —Sister Patterson

Samuel folded the note carefully and placed it in his Bible next to the Habakkuk passage. Some sermons wrote themselves in moments like these, when the theology of waiting met the reality of love made practical.

By mid-morning, the lot bustled with the organized activity that had become Mount Zion's signature. The women's auxiliary had transformed the shade under the old oak tree into a outdoor kitchen, complete with tables made from sawhorses and boards, a wash station fashioned from galvanized tubs, and a serving line that could feed a small army on short notice.

What had begun as a simple plan to provide lunch for the volunteer construction workers had evolved into something larger and more significant: a community feeding program that served anyone who arrived hungry, no questions asked, no sermons required, just the simple understanding that food was love made tangible.

Essie stood at the center of the operation, directing traffic with the calm authority of a conductor leading a familiar symphony. To her left, Mother Caldwell stirred a pot of beans that had been simmering since dawn, seasoned with ham hocks donated by James from the rail yard and wisdom accumulated over seven decades of making much from little. To her right, Ruth carefully arranged squares of cornbread on plates, each portion measured with the mathematical precision of someone who understood that fairness meant everyone got fed, even if the portions were modest.

"Ruth, honey, make sure that cornbread gets to the children first," Essie called without looking up from the large pot of greens she was tending. "Growing bodies need the nourishment more than grown folks do."

Ruth nodded and began carrying plates toward the corner of the lot where a small group of neighborhood children had gathered. They came from families where lunch was sometimes a luxury, where parents worked jobs that paid too little to cover all the necessities and left children to fend for themselves during the long hours between breakfast and supper.

Among the children was a boy Ruth recognized from Sunday school, though his attendance had become sporadic as his family's circumstances became more difficult. His name was Daniel, and he had the particular thinness that came not from activity but from meals missed, clothes that hung loose on a frame that should have been filling out with the sturdy growth of childhood.

"Hey, Daniel," Ruth said, offering him a plate with an extra square of cornbread. "How you been? Haven't seen you at church lately."

Daniel accepted the plate with the careful politeness of a child who had learned not to take charity for granted. "Been helping Mama with the baby while she works. Can't leave little Sarah by herself, and we can't afford nobody to watch her."

Ruth felt something tighten in her chest, a recognition of the impossible mathematics that forced children to become adults before their time, that made Sunday worship a luxury when survival demanded every available hour. She thought of her own comfortable routine—Sunday school followed by service, dinner around the family table, afternoons free for play and study.

"Maybe the baby could come to Sunday school too," she suggested. "We got women who love holding babies, and they could help watch her while your mama's at service."

Daniel's face brightened with a hope that was immediately tempered by practical concerns. "Mama says we can't be a burden on church folks. Says we got to handle our own troubles."

"That's not troubles, that's family," Ruth replied with the conviction of someone repeating words she had heard from her parents countless times. "Church family helps church family. That's what family does."

As the lunch service continued, Samuel moved among the gathering crowd with the easy familiarity of a pastor who understood that ministry happened as much in casual conversations as in formal sermons. He stopped to talk with Moses about the progress on the window frames, checked with James about the delivery of roofing materials they still couldn't quite afford, and listened with patient attention to Mrs. Henderson's concerns about her husband's persistent cough.

But his attention was drawn to a commotion near the street, where a small group of men had gathered around someone Samuel didn't immediately recognize. The stranger was clearly agitated, gesturing with hands that shook with either fear or exhaustion, his voice carrying the particular urgency of someone delivering news that couldn't wait for proper introductions.

Samuel approached the group, and the conversation quieted as the men deferred to their pastor's presence. The stranger was young, perhaps twenty-five, with the lean build of a fieldworker and clothes that spoke of hard travel and harder circumstances. His eyes held the haunted quality Samuel had learned to recognize—the look of someone who had seen violence up close and personal.

"This is Marcus," James explained, placing a steadying hand on the stranger's shoulder. "He walked all night from over near the county line. Got some news about the Hendricks family."

Samuel's stomach tightened. The Hendricks family had been members of Mount Zion for two years, ever since moving down from Virginia in search of work and a fresh start. Tom Hendricks had found employment at the sawmill, and his wife Mary had taken in sewing to supplement their income. They had three children, including a baby born just that spring.

"Tom tried to organize the mill workers," Marcus said, his words coming in rushed bursts as if he feared losing his nerve before the story was complete. "Nothing radical, just asking for fair wages and safer conditions. But the mill owner, he didn't see it that way. Claimed Tom was stirring up trouble, making the other workers lazy and demanding."

Samuel felt the familiar chill that came when individual stories intersected with larger systems of injustice, when good people found themselves caught in machinery designed to grind hope into submission.

"Where are they now?" Samuel asked, though he suspected the answer would be complicated.

"That's the thing, Pastor. They had to leave. Tom got word that some of the owner's friends were planning a visit to his house, the kind of visit that comes at night with ropes and no intention of conversation. They packed what they could carry and left before dawn yesterday."

The implications settled over the group like dust from a passing wagon. The Hendricks family had been contributing members of the Mount Zion community, their children in Sunday school, their voices part of the choir, their small but steady offerings helping to fund the building project. More than that, they represented the kind of people the church was being built for—working families looking for dignity, community, and a chance to raise their children in safety.

"You know where they went?" Moses asked.

Marcus shook his head. "Tom said something about heading north, maybe to Baltimore where Mary's got a sister. But they didn't have much money, and traveling with three little ones..." He let the sentence trail off, leaving unsaid the dozens of ways such a journey could end badly.

Samuel closed his eyes and offered a brief, silent prayer for the Hendricks family's safety and for wisdom about how to respond to their situation. When he opened them, he found the circle of men looking at him with the expectation that had become both a blessing and a burden—the assumption that the preacher would know what to do when the world showed its cruel face.

"We pray for their protection," he said finally. "And we remember that building this church isn't just about having a place to worship on Sunday mornings. It's about creating sanctuary for folks like the Hendricks, people who need a community that will stand with them when standing becomes dangerous."

James nodded slowly. "Makes you wonder who's next. Mill owner gets away with running off one family for asking fair questions, he might decide to make examples of others."

"Then we make sure there are others," Samuel replied with quiet intensity. "We build this church, we build this community, we create a place where working folks can find their voice and know they won't have to use it alone."

The conversation was interrupted by the sound of automobile engines approaching from the direction of town. Two black cars moved slowly down the street, their occupants visible through the windows but not immediately identifiable. The vehicles passed the lot without stopping, but their presence felt like a statement, a reminder that the work happening at Mount Zion was being observed and evaluated by parties unknown.

"Speaking of standing together," Moses muttered, watching the cars disappear around the corner.

Samuel felt the weight of leadership settling on his shoulders like a heavy coat. Every decision carried implications that rippled beyond his own family, beyond his own congregation, into a community where the wrong choice could endanger lives and the right choice might require risking everything they had worked to build.

But as he looked around the lot—at the women serving meals to hungry children, at the men discussing construction plans and community concerns, at Ruth helping Daniel find a comfortable place to sit while he ate his lunch—Samuel felt something stronger than fear. He felt the presence of what Mother Caldwell called "the Lord's stubborn grace," the divine tendency to plant hope in the most unlikely soil and nurture it with the most improbable resources.

"We keep building," he said, addressing the circle of men but speaking loudly enough for anyone nearby to hear. "We keep feeding folks who need feeding, we keep welcoming families who need welcoming, and we keep believing that love is stronger than fear, even when fear comes driving down the street in black cars with tinted windows."

The men nodded, not with the easy confidence of those who had never faced real danger, but with the settled determination of those who had weighed the costs and chosen their side anyway. The conversation gradually turned back to practical matters—who would deliver supplies to the Hendricks family if their location could be discovered, how to strengthen the networks of communication that kept the community informed of threats and opportunities, what scripture passages might speak to the current situation.

But Samuel's attention drifted toward the unfinished frame of Mount Zion, where afternoon shadows were beginning to gather between the support beams. The church looked vulnerable in the slanted light, exposed and incomplete. Yet something about its very openness seemed intentional now, as if the lack of walls was not a deficiency but a design feature, an invitation rather than an oversight.

A sanctuary, he realized, was not primarily about keeping danger out. It was about keeping hope alive inside, even when—especially when—the outside world seemed determined to extinguish it.

The afternoon brought unexpected grace in the form of an envelope that appeared during the lunch service without fanfare or explanation. Ruth discovered it tucked under the corner of one of the serving tables, addressed simply to "Mount Zion Building Fund" in handwriting that was careful but unfamiliar.

She carried it to her father, who was helping Moses align a window frame that had been giving them trouble all morning. The carpentry work provided a welcome distraction from the morning's troubling news about the Hendricks family, the kind of physical problem that could be solved with patience, measurements, and the proper application of tools.

"Daddy, somebody left this," Ruth said, holding out the envelope with the reverence she had learned to show toward anything connected to the church building project.

Samuel set down his level and wiped his hands on his work pants before accepting the envelope. It was ordinary in every way—cheap paper, no return address, the kind of envelope that could be purchased at any general store for a few cents. But there was something about its very anonymity that made it feel significant, like a message from a source that preferred to remain hidden.

Inside were five twenty-dollar bills and a note written on plain paper in the same careful handwriting:

For the roof of Mount Zion Baptist Church. From a friend who believes in what you're building. May the Lord bless the work of your hands.

Samuel stared at the bills as if they might disappear if he looked away. One hundred dollars represented more than most working families saw in two months, enough to purchase a significant portion of the roofing materials they needed to protect the building through the coming winter.

"Moses," he called, his voice carrying a note of amazement that drew immediate attention. "Come look at this."

Moses set down his hammer and walked over, his expression shifting from casual interest to stunned recognition as he saw the money in Samuel's hands. "Lord have mercy," he whispered. "Where'd that come from?"

"Good question," Samuel replied, looking around the lot as if the mysterious benefactor might still be present, identifiable by some telltale sign of generosity. "Ruth found it under the serving table, but nobody saw who put it there."

Word of the mysterious gift spread through the gathering with the speed that significant news always traveled in small communities. Work stopped as people gathered around to examine the evidence of what could only be described as divine intervention, or at least divine timing. The amount was too large to have come from any single member of their congregation, too precisely targeted to be coincidental.

"Could be somebody from outside the community," Essie suggested, her practical mind working through the possibilities. "Maybe someone who's heard about what we're doing and wants to help but doesn't want recognition."

Mother Caldwell, who had been stirring her pot of beans with the steady rhythm of someone lost in thought, looked up with the particular expression she wore when larger patterns were becoming clear to her. "Could be the Lord working through somebody who's got means but not the courage to give openly," she said. "Fear makes people do charity in the shadows sometimes."

Samuel folded the money carefully and slipped it into his shirt pocket, close to his heart. "Whoever it was, they just answered a prayer we been carrying for months. This is enough to get the roof started, maybe finished if we're careful with the spending."

The news energized the entire gathering. Men who had been working with the steady resignation of those tackling an impossible task suddenly moved with the quick efficiency of those who could see the finish line. Women who had been serving meals with quiet determination began to hum as they worked, their songs carrying the lightness that comes when burdens unexpectedly become manageable.

Ruth found herself thinking about seeds again—not the turnip green seeds she had distributed months earlier, but the less tangible seeds that were planted every time someone chose generosity over fear, community over isolation, hope over the easier mathematics of despair. The anonymous gift felt like a harvest from seeds planted by countless small acts of faithfulness, a return on investments that had been made without expectation of profit.

As the afternoon work continued, the mysterious donation became woven into the ongoing story of Mount Zion's construction, another chapter in the accumulating evidence that the church was being built by more hands than those that held hammers, funded by more hearts than those that openly contributed to the building fund.

Samuel found himself returning repeatedly to the biblical account of the widow's mite, the story Jesus told about the poor woman who gave everything she had while rich men made shows of their larger but less costly contributions. But today the story seemed to be running in reverse—instead of small gifts that carried great meaning, they had received a large gift that carried the humility of the small, an offering made in secret rather than display.

By evening, as the volunteers began to clean up their tools and pack away the remnants of the lunch service, the lot buzzed with a renewed energy that had been missing since the summer's initial enthusiasm had given way to autumn's grinding reality. The anonymous donation had provided more than money—it had restored the sense that they were not building alone, that their small community of faith was connected to a larger network of people who believed in the vision of sanctuary.

Samuel stood at the edge of the lot as the last of the volunteers headed home, watching the sun set behind the frame of Mount Zion. The building looked different now, not just because of the money in his pocket but because of what that money represented—proof that the work they were doing mattered to people beyond their immediate circle, evidence that hope was contagious and could spread in ways they might never fully understand.

Essie joined him, slipping her hand into his as they surveyed the day's progress. "Good day," she said with the satisfaction of someone who had witnessed small miracles become practical blessings.

"Very good day," Samuel agreed. "Makes a person wonder what other surprises the Lord might have in store."

"Long as they keep coming in envelopes instead of black cars, I'm ready for whatever surprises want to show up," Essie replied with the wry humor that had kept their marriage strong through twenty years of uncertainty and hope mixed in equal measure.

As they walked toward the house, Ruth skipped ahead of them, her spirit light with the particular joy that comes from being present when adults' prayers are answered in ways that restore their faith in the goodness of strangers. Behind them, Mount Zion's frame stood silhouetted against the evening sky, no longer looking quite so vulnerable, no longer seeming quite so impossible.

The roof would come. The walls would rise. The sanctuary would be completed. And somewhere in the growing darkness, the anonymous friend who had made it possible was probably saying their own prayers of gratitude, blessed by the opportunity to participate in the ancient work of turning visions into reality, one act of faithfulness at a time.

The sound came at three in the morning—not the sharp crack of breaking wood or the crash of something falling, but the low, steady roar of fire consuming dry timber. Samuel woke to the smell of smoke drifting through the bedroom window and the distant glow of flames painting the night sky the wrong color.

He was out of bed and pulling on his pants before full consciousness arrived, moving with the automatic efficiency of someone who had lived through enough emergencies to know that the gap between recognizing danger and responding to it could mean the difference between salvage and total loss. Essie sat up in bed, instantly alert in the way of mothers who had learned to parse the significance of nighttime sounds.

"Fire," Samuel said, confirming what they both already knew. Through the window, they could see the orange glow that transformed familiar neighborhood landmarks into strange, flickering shapes. The light was coming from the direction of Mount Zion.

They dressed quickly and in silence, the practiced teamwork of a couple who had learned to move together through crisis. Ruth appeared in the hallway, rubbing sleep from her eyes but already reaching for the clothes her mother was handing her. No one had to explain the urgency; the smell of smoke and the wrong light in the sky provided all the motivation they needed.

Outside, the night air carried the acrid scent of burning wood and something else—the particular chemical smell of paint or stain being consumed by flames. Samuel's heart clenched as he saw the source of the fire: Mount Zion's frame engulfed in flames that rose like angry prayers toward the stars.

The lot was already crowded with neighbors who had been drawn from their homes by the same smoke and light that had awakened the Washington family. Some carried buckets, though the fire was clearly beyond what bucket brigades could handle. Others simply stood and watched, their faces reflecting the flames and the particular helplessness that comes when months of work disappear in minutes.

Samuel ran toward the burning structure, stopped only by Moses's strong hand on his shoulder. "Nothing to save, Pastor," Moses said, his voice carrying the weight of practical assessment and personal grief. "She's gone."

The flames had consumed not just the wooden frame but everything that represented months of hope made manifest. The careful measurements, the level corners, the hand-selected lumber—all of it feeding a fire that seemed to dance with malevolent joy. The heat was intense enough to keep the crowd well back from the structure, turning witnesses into helpless observers of destruction they could not prevent or even meaningfully fight.

Essie moved through the crowd with quiet efficiency, checking on elderly neighbors who had been awakened by the commotion, making sure children stayed safely away from the heat and flying sparks, offering the practical comfort that was her particular gift. But Samuel noticed that she avoided looking directly at the fire, as if watching their dreams burn might somehow make the destruction more complete.

Ruth stood between her parents, her small hand gripping Samuel's with the fierce intensity of someone trying to anchor him to the ground when everything solid seemed to be disappearing. She had never seen anything she cared about destroyed so completely and so quickly. The church frame had been a constant presence in her life for months, a promise taking shape board by board, nail by nail. Now it was becoming memory even as she watched.

"Who would do this?" she asked, her voice small but clear enough to carry to the adults nearby.

The question hung in the smoky air like an accusation. Everyone present understood that this fire was not accidental—the flames were too evenly distributed, too complete in their consumption, too conveniently timed to be anything but deliberate.

Someone had decided that Mount Zion represented a threat that needed to be eliminated.

James arrived carrying a bucket of water, took one look at the inferno, and set the bucket down with the resignation of someone who had lived long enough to recognize hopeless situations. "Volunteer fire department won't get here for another hour," he said. "Even if they came right now, wouldn't be much left to save."

Samuel nodded, his eyes fixed on the flames that were consuming not just wood but the accumulated faith of a community that had believed in the possibility of building something beautiful in a world that seemed determined to destroy beauty wherever it appeared. The anonymous donation that had arrived just that afternoon—the hundred dollars that was going to pay for the roof—felt like cosmic mockery now that there was nothing left to roof.

But as he watched the fire burn, Samuel felt something unexpected rising in his chest. Not despair, though despair would have been justified. Not anger, though anger would have been understandable. Instead, he felt a stubborn certainty that whoever had set this fire had fundamentally misunderstood what they were trying to destroy.

"They burned the frame," he said, speaking to no one in particular but loud enough for everyone to hear. "But they can't burn the vision. They can't burn what we learned about working together. They can't burn the bonds we built while we were building the building."

Mother Caldwell's voice rose from her place in the crowd, carrying the authority of someone who had survived decades of attempts to extinguish hope through violence: "That's right, Pastor. Fire burns wood, but it can't touch faith. And it sure can't touch what the Lord has planned."

As if in response to her words, the main support beam of the church frame crashed down in a shower of sparks that rose toward the stars like offerings being returned to heaven. The sound was both ending and beginning—the final collapse of one vision and the first stirring of something that might replace it.

Samuel turned to face the crowd of neighbors and church members who had gathered to witness the destruction. In their faces, he saw the reflection of his own complex emotions—grief for what was lost, anger at what had been taken, but underneath it all, the stubborn resilience that had brought their families through slavery, Reconstruction, and decades of systematic attempts to convince them they had no right to build anything worth preserving.

"Tomorrow morning," he said, his voice carrying easily despite the crackle of flames, "we're going to come back to this lot. We're going to clear away what can't be saved, and we're going to start over. Because that's what we do. That's who we are. We build, and when someone tears down what we built, we build again."

Essie moved to stand beside him, her presence a reminder that he did not carry the burden of leadership alone. "Takes more than fire to stop the Lord's work," she said, her words carrying the practical faith that had sustained her through twenty years of marriage to a man who insisted on believing that impossible things could become possible through stubborn persistence and divine grace.

The fire burned for another two hours, consuming every piece of lumber they had so carefully selected and placed. When the flames finally died down to glowing embers, nothing remained of Mount Zion but the foundation stones and the memory of what had been built there. Even the tools that had been stored in the makeshift lean-to were gone, metal twisted by heat into shapes that would never again drive nails or measure boards.

But as the crowd finally began to disperse toward homes that now felt more precious for being intact, Samuel noticed something that the fire had not touched: the old oak tree under which the women's auxiliary had served so many meals still stood unharmed, its branches creating a canopy of shade that would welcome them back when morning came.

The foundation stones, too, remained solid and level, ready to support whatever structure might rise to replace what had been destroyed. And in Samuel's shirt pocket, the anonymous donation that had arrived just that afternoon waited to fund not a roof but a resurrection, not completion but a new beginning that might prove even stronger for having been tested by flames.

As Ruth walked home between her parents, she found herself thinking not about what they had lost but about what remained: the community that had gathered so quickly when crisis called, the determination that had declared itself even while the embers still glowed, the stubborn insistence that building was stronger than burning, that hope was more durable than hate.

Behind them, Mount Zion's foundation stones gleamed like a promise in the starlight, patient as the faith that had laid them, ready as the dawn that would surely come.

Dawn arrived gray and subdued, as if the sky itself was in mourning for what had been lost. Samuel stood at the kitchen window, watching the smoke rise in thin tendrils from the lot where Mount Zion had stood. The fire was out, but the smell of burned wood lingered in the air like incense from a service no one had wanted to attend.

Essie moved quietly around the kitchen, preparing coffee and breakfast with the careful attention to routine that helped maintain normalcy when the world felt turned upside down. Ruth sat at the table, her usually animated morning energy subdued by the weight of witnessing destruction she was still too young to fully understand.

"How long will it take to build again?" she asked, her voice carrying the particular hopefulness of children who believe that adult determination can solve any problem, given enough time and effort.

Samuel turned from the window and settled into his chair at the table, accepting the coffee Essie poured with hands that were steadier than his heart. The question was reasonable, but the answer was complicated by mathematics that went beyond construction schedules to encompass the psychology of a community that had invested everything in a dream and watched it burn.

"Well," he said carefully, "building goes faster when you already know what you're doing. We learned a lot the first time around—how to lay foundation, how to frame walls, how to work together. That knowledge doesn't burn."

Essie set a plate of eggs and biscuits in front of him, the food representing normalcy and care in a morning when both felt precious and fragile. "The foundation stones are still good," she added, picking up the thread of practical optimism. "And we still got that hundred dollars that came in yesterday. The Lord's timing on that gift feels mighty significant this morning."

Through the window, Samuel could see neighbors beginning to gather on the lot, drawn by the same impulse that had brought them there in crisis the night before. Some carried tools, others brought buckets and rakes, all of them moving with the determined purpose of people who had decided that destruction would not have the last word.

"Looks like we won't be clearing the debris by ourselves," Samuel observed, watching James and Moses examining the foundation stones, testing their integrity after the heat of the fire. "Folks are already showing up to help."

By the time the Washington family finished breakfast and walked across the street to the lot, the cleanup effort was well underway. The twisted remains of the church frame lay in charred piles, but willing hands were already sorting through the debris, separating what might be salvaged from what needed to be hauled away.

Mother Caldwell had established herself in her usual chair under the oak tree, though this morning her role was less supervisory than ministerial. She greeted each arriving volunteer with words of encouragement, dispensed wisdom about the spiritual significance of rebuilding, and maintained a steady stream of commentary that kept spirits up and hands busy.

"Fire may have burned the building," she announced to no one in particular and everyone in general, "but it purified the ground. Sometimes the Lord has to clear away the old before the new can come forth in all its glory."

Ruth found herself drawn to the foundation stones, which remained remarkably intact despite the intense heat they had endured. She ran her small hands along the mortar joints, checking for cracks or damage, relieved to find them solid and true. These stones had been laid with her father's hands, blessed with her community's prayers, and they had survived destruction to offer themselves as the base for whatever would come next.

"The foundation held," she reported to Samuel with the solemnity of a building inspector delivering crucial findings.

"Of course it did," Samuel replied, kneeling beside her to examine the stones himself. "We built it to last. Built it with the kind of faith that doesn't burn, the kind of hope that gets stronger when it's tested."

As the morning progressed, the lot began to transform from a scene of destruction into something that looked increasingly like preparation for new construction. The debris was cleared, the foundation was cleaned and inspected, and volunteers began discussing plans that were ambitious in ways that surprised even Samuel.

"Seems to me," James said during a break in the cleanup work, "that whoever burned the first church did us a favor in one respect. Now we know how much support we got in this community. Look around—we got more people here today than we ever had during the original building."

Samuel looked around and realized James was right. The fire had drawn not only the core members of Mount Zion but also neighbors who had never attended services, community members who had watched the building project with quiet interest, and even a few faces he didn't recognize at all—people who had been moved by news of the fire to offer assistance to strangers.

Among the volunteers was Mrs. Patterson from Elm Street, the same woman who had contributed her carefully saved dollars and whose turnip greens had grown from Ruth's seed packets. She worked with quiet efficiency, sweeping debris from the foundation stones, her presence a reminder that the church being rebuilt would serve a community larger than its formal membership.

"Mrs. Patterson," Samuel said, approaching her during a lull in the work, "I want to thank you for being here. I know you got your own responsibilities to tend to."

She paused in her sweeping and looked at him with eyes that held the particular wisdom of someone who had survived multiple disappointments without losing the capacity for hope. "Pastor Washington," she said, "this church was being built for folks like me, wasn't it? Folks who need a place to belong, a community that believes in building up instead of tearing down?"

"Yes ma'am, it was."

"Then I got just as much stake in seeing it rise again as anybody else. Maybe more, since I still got turnip greens growing in my yard from seeds that came from this ministry."

As the day wore on, the cleanup work revealed not just the extent of the damage but the unexpected gifts that destruction had uncovered. Buried beneath the charred remains of the support beams, Moses discovered a metal box that had somehow survived the fire. Inside, wrapped in oilcloth, were the original building plans Samuel had sketched months earlier, along with photographs of the construction process and a list of every person who had contributed to the building fund.

"Look here," Moses called, his voice carrying a note of wonder that drew everyone's attention. "The fire couldn't touch everything."

Samuel accepted the box with hands that trembled slightly, understanding that he was holding more than papers and pictures—he was holding the accumulated memory of their shared work, the documented proof that what they had built together was worth building again. The photographs showed faces bright with hope and hands busy with purpose, a visual record of community in action.

"We'll need these for the new building," he said, his voice growing stronger with each word. "Same plans, but better. Stronger. Built with everything we learned the first time and everything we're learning right now about what it means to stand together when standing gets dangerous."

Mother Caldwell's voice rose from her chair under the oak, carrying the tone she used for pronouncements that brooked no disagreement: "The Lord works in mysterious ways, but sometimes the ways ain't so mysterious. Sometimes they just stubborn. Same as the people the Lord chooses to work through."

By afternoon, the lot looked nothing like the scene of devastation they had encountered at dawn. The debris was cleared, the foundation was cleaned, and several volunteers had already begun discussing the logistics of ordering new lumber. More significantly, the cleanup had become a planning session, with ideas flowing as freely as the sweet tea Mother Caldwell had organized the women to serve.

"This time we build with brick on the lower level," suggested James, his experience with railroad construction informing his recommendations. "Won't burn so easy, and it'll look more permanent. Show folks we're here to stay."

"And we need better security," added Moses, his voice carrying the weight of practical concerns that no one wanted to voice directly but everyone had been thinking about. "Way to protect the building when we're not here to watch over it."

Samuel listened to the suggestions with the growing awareness that the fire had accomplished something the arsonist never intended: it had unified the community around the building project in ways that simple enthusiasm never could. The destruction had clarified what mattered, had sorted the merely curious from the genuinely committed, had transformed individual interest into collective determination.

"We'll need to raise more money," Essie pointed out with her characteristic attention to practical realities. "Brick costs more than lumber, and we'll need everything we had before plus what these new ideas require."

"Money will come," Mother Caldwell declared with the confidence of someone who had seen divine provision operate through unexpected channels for seven decades. "Money always comes when the Lord has work that needs doing. Might not come when we expect it or how we expect it, but it comes."

As if summoned by her words, a figure approached from the direction of town—a woman walking with the measured pace of someone carrying important news. As she drew closer, Samuel recognized her as Mrs. Thompson, who worked as a domestic for one of the prominent white families on the north side of town.

"Pastor Washington," she called as she reached the edge of the crowd. "I got a message for you. From Mrs. Elizabeth Morrison."

Samuel felt a slight chill at the name. The Morrison family owned significant property in the county, including the bank where several Mount Zion members maintained accounts and the general store where most of the community did their shopping. If Mrs. Morrison had sent a message, it carried weight that extended far beyond personal communication.

Mrs. Thompson reached into her apron and withdrew an envelope, this one clearly expensive paper with elegant handwriting. "She heard about the fire. Asked me to bring this by and tell you that she was sorry for your loss."

Samuel accepted the envelope with the careful attention he had learned to give to communications from powerful white families. Such messages could contain anything from genuine sympathy to veiled threats, and the difference often lay not in the words chosen but in the circumstances surrounding their delivery.

Inside was a brief note written in the precise script of someone who had received extensive education in an era when such education was rare for anyone, especially women:

Pastor Washington—I was distressed to learn of the fire that destroyed your church building. While I did not know your congregation personally, I have observed your community's dedication to the building project and have been impressed by the dignity and persistence with which the work has been conducted. Please accept the enclosed contribution toward your rebuilding effort, given in memory of my late husband who believed that houses of worship, regardless of denomination, serve essential purposes in maintaining the moral fabric of our community. —Mrs. Elizabeth Morrison

Samuel opened the folded paper that had been tucked inside the note and found himself staring at a bank draft for five hundred dollars—more money than Mount Zion's building fund had ever contained, more than most of their members earned in a year, enough to rebuild the church with the brick construction James had suggested and perhaps even add some of the improvements they had only dreamed about.

"Lord have mercy," Moses whispered when Samuel showed him the draft. "That woman just handed us more money than we ever asked the Lord to provide."

The news of Mrs. Morrison's contribution spread through the crowd with the speed that extraordinary developments always traveled in small communities. Some volunteers were amazed by the generosity, others puzzled by the motivation, and a few concerned about what strings might be attached to such largesse from unexpected sources.

"Why would she do that?" Ruth asked, her young mind working to understand the social dynamics that would motivate a wealthy white woman to support the rebuilding of a Black church she had never visited.

Samuel folded the bank draft carefully and slipped it into his shirt pocket next to the anonymous hundred-dollar contribution that had arrived the day before. "Maybe because some people understand that building up is better than tearing down, regardless of who's doing the building," he said. "Maybe because goodness recognizes goodness, even across the lines folks draw to separate themselves from each other."

Mother Caldwell rocked forward in her chair, her voice taking on the particular tone she used for observations that connected immediate circumstances to eternal principles: "The Lord moves in mysterious ways, but sometimes the ways ain't mysterious at all. Sometimes they just slow. Plant seeds of goodness, and you never know what ground they might take root in or when they might bloom into something beautiful."

As the afternoon shadows lengthened across the lot, the volunteers began to pack up their tools and prepare to return to evening routines of cooking and family care. But the energy of the day had transformed what could have been a community defeated by arson into a community energized by the possibility of building something better than what had been destroyed.

Samuel stood among the foundation stones as the last volunteers headed home, holding bank drafts that represented more financial support than he had dared to pray for, surrounded by evidence of community solidarity that exceeded his most optimistic expectations. The fire had been intended to end their story, but instead it had written a new chapter—one that began not with destruction but with resurrection, not with fear but with the stubborn insistence that hope could not be burned down by people who mistook buildings for the faith that raised them.

Essie joined him as the evening sky darkened over the lot that would soon hold the third iteration of Mount Zion Baptist Church. "Feels different this time, doesn't it?" she said, slipping her hand into his as they surveyed the clean foundation that waited patiently for new walls to rise.

"Feels like the Lord was just waiting for us to be ready for what was really possible," Samuel replied. "Feels like the fire cleared away more than just lumber—cleared away our small thinking, our careful hoping, our fear of dreaming too big."

Behind them, the oak tree that had sheltered their community meals spread its branches like arms raised in blessing over the lot where their sanctuary would rise again.

Marching Orders

The spiritual "We Shall Overcome" rose from beyond the bathroom door, steady and certain as a river finding its course. Ruth Washington pressed her ear against the wood, listening to voices joined in harmony—determination carried in every note, shaped by years of waiting. She heard it in the way they held the final syllables, the way the melody refused to waver even as footsteps shuffled and chairs scraped against linoleum. These were voices that had earned the right to claim victory before victory was visible, singing at the Woolworth's lunch counter where she would soon join them.

She was twenty-five now. A schoolteacher. Her childhood braids were gone, replaced by careful styling that marked her as an adult woman of substance in the community. But standing in that cramped bathroom, waiting for the signal that would launch her into direct action—the kind her father had spent years preparing for through prayer and patience—she felt young again. Uncertain. Like the girl who had once scattered seeds in hostile neighborhoods.

The plan was simple in the way that acts of courage often were: she and fifteen other members of Mount Zion Baptist Church would walk out of this bathroom, take seats at the lunch counter that had never served Black customers, and order coffee and pie with the quiet dignity that was their birthright and the system's greatest fear. They would sit until they were served or until they were arrested, whichever came first. Either outcome would advance the cause.

Ruth checked her appearance in the cracked mirror above the sink—white blouse pressed crisp as her resolve, dark skirt that wouldn't show dirt if she ended up on the ground, low shoes that would let her walk with dignity whether the walk led to a cell or back to the street. She had dressed like her mother had taught her to dress for church, because this too was a form of worship, a way of bearing witness to the truth that all of God's children deserved equal treatment at every table.

Through the door, she could hear the lunch counter growing quiet as the singing stopped and the real work began. Her heart hammered against her ribs.

, but her hands were steady. Months of preparation had gone into this moment—strategy sessions in church basements, nonviolence training led by organizers who had learned their lessons in Birmingham and Montgomery, prayers offered by parents who understood that their children were about to risk everything for the possibility of change.

The door opened and Keisha Daniels peered in, her face set with determination—time to move.

Keisha was Ruth's closest friend and her partner in the kind of idealism that drove young women to believe they could change the world through the simple act of refusing to accept injustice as permanent.

"You ready?" Keisha whispered, though her tone suggested she already knew the answer.

They walked out of the bathroom together, Ruth's heels clicking against the linoleum floor with a rhythm that sounded like determination made audible. The lunch counter stretched ahead of them like a bridge between the world they had inherited and the world they intended to create for their children. Red vinyl stools stood in a neat row, each one representing a small revolution waiting to happen.

The white customers at the counter looked up as Ruth and Keisha approached, their faces changing: surprise, then confusion, then something harder.

The waitress—a middle-aged woman whose uniform suggested years of experience serving customers who looked nothing like the two young Black women now claiming seats—froze with a coffee pot in her hand as if time itself had stuttered.

"Good morning," Ruth said with the careful politeness her parents had drilled into her since childhood. "Could we please have two cups of coffee and a slice of apple pie to share?"

The silence that followed was thick enough to cut.

. Ruth could feel the attention of every person in the store focusing on the lunch counter like heat from a magnifying glass, could sense the shift in atmosphere that came when daily routine collided with historical change.

"We don't serve your kind here," the waitress said finally, her words carrying less malice than weary inevitability, as if she were reciting lines from a script she had never chosen but was required to perform.

"We're customers, same as anyone else," Keisha replied, her voice carrying the particular steadiness that came from months of practicing this exact conversation in church basements and living rooms. "We'd like to place an order, please."

I understand you want me to remove editorial markup from a text, but I don't see any actual narrative text provided in your message. The content you've shared appears to be entirely editorial/meta-commentary about a missing text.

Could you please provide the actual Chapter 4 narrative text that contains the editorial markup you'd like removed? I'm ready to help once I can see the story content itself.

The manager appeared, his face flushed with the kind of anger that came when established order met organized resistance. Other customers began to leave, some shaking their heads in disgust, others casting backward glances that mixed curiosity with concern. The lunch counter became a stage where decades of social convention played out their final act.

"You need to leave," the manager said, his voice tight with the control required to avoid saying what he really thought. "This establishment reserves the right to refuse service."

"We're not asking for special treatment," Ruth said, maintaining the tone of reasonable conversation even as her pulse quickened. "Just the same service offered to every other customer."

The argument that followed was less debate than ritual, each side reciting positions that had been rehearsed in courtrooms and churches, in newspapers and night meetings, in the careful preparation that preceded every act of nonviolent resistance. Ruth found herself thinking of her father's sermons about patience, about the appointed time when justice would roll down like water. But sitting on that vinyl stool, feeling the weight of history settling on her shoulders like a mantle, she wondered if perhaps the appointed time had arrived not through divine intervention but through human determination to stop waiting and start demanding.

The police arrived within fifteen minutes, their uniforms representing the enforcement arm of laws that Ruth and her companions had decided were fundamentally unjust. The officers were polite in the way that Southern law enforcement had learned to be polite when cameras might be present and northern newspapers might be watching. They explained the charges—trespassing, disturbing the peace, interfering with business operations—with the professional courtesy that made injustice sound reasonable.

Ruth stood from her stool with the same dignity she had been practicing since childhood, the same composed bearing her mother had modeled during decades of navigating a world that questioned her right to exist in spaces she helped maintain through her labor. The handcuffs were cold against her wrists, but the touch of metal could not diminish the warmth she felt from the other demonstrators who rose with her, who walked toward the police cars with the measured pace of people who understood they were participating in something larger than a lunch counter protest.

As they were loaded into the police cars, Ruth caught a glimpse of the crowd that had gathered outside Woolworth's. Some faces showed support—subtle nods, small smiles, the kind of encouragement that had to be given carefully in a town where being seen on the wrong side could cost jobs, homes, safety. But other faces showed the particular hardness that came when change arrived faster than some people were prepared to accept it.

The jail was not her first time in a cell—months of civil rights activity had familiarized her with the routine of booking, fingerprinting, and the particular humiliation of being processed like a criminal for demanding basic human dignity. But tonight felt different, weighted with significance that went beyond individual protest to something that might actually shift the foundations of how business was conducted in their small North Carolina town.

In the cell she shared with Keisha and two other demonstrators, Ruth found herself thinking about the distance between the girl who had scattered seed packets in hostile neighborhoods and the woman who now sat in jail for refusing to accept that lunch counters had racial restrictions. The journey felt both long and short, measured not in years but in moments when small acts of courage accumulated into the kind of momentum that could move mountains.

"You think it worked?" Keisha asked, her voice carrying the exhaustion that came after the adrenaline of direct action gave way to the reality of consequences.

"Depends on what you mean by worked," Ruth replied, settling back against the cell wall that had held countless other people who had chosen principle over peace. "If you mean did we get served coffee and pie, then no. But if you mean did we make it impossible for them to pretend the lunch counter isn't a problem, then yes."

Through the small window of their cell, Ruth could see the evening sky darkening over the town where she had been born and raised, where her parents had built a church from nothing but faith and stubborn determination, where her own children might someday grow up in a world where lunch counters served everyone equally. The distance between might and will stretched like a bridge she was helping to build, one act of nonviolent resistance at a time.

The sound of singing drifted through the jail from other cells, other voices that had chosen arrest over acceptance of injustice. The spiritual that rose through the corridors was the same one that had sustained her people through slavery, Reconstruction, and decades of systematic oppression designed to convince them they deserved less than full participation in American life. But tonight the song carried a different note, the sound of patience giving way to insistence, of waiting being transformed into acting.

Ruth added her voice to the chorus. The melody moved from cell to cell, women's voices joining together in the close darkness. Through the high window, she could see a single star.

Tomorrow there would be bail hearings and newspaper articles, strategy meetings and the careful planning that turned individual acts of courage into sustained movements for change. But tonight there was only the singing, the fellowship of people who had decided that some principles were worth sleeping on jail cots for, worth risking everything for the possibility that their children might inherit a more just world.

As the singing continued, Ruth felt something settle in her chest that she recognized as the same stubborn faith that had built Mount Zion Baptist Church from foundation stones and community dreams. The lunch counter protest was part of the same work—building something better from the materials of courage and hope, refusing to let fear have the final word in conversations about dignity and belonging.

Outside, the town continued its evening routine, but inside the jail cells where civil rights demonstrators waited for morning, a different kind of evening prayer was being offered—not the kind that asked for divine intervention, but the kind that declared human intention to participate in their own liberation, one lunch counter at a time.

The phone rang at dawn.

Ruth rolled over in bed.

. Ruth rolled over in bed, reaching for the phone with the automatic efficiency of someone who had learned to parse the meaning of early morning calls—emergency, crisis, or the kind of news that couldn't wait for decent hours.

"Ruth?" The voice belonged to James from Mount Zion, but it carried a strain she had never heard before, the particular tightness that came when strong men found themselves delivering news that tested the limits of their strength. "You need to come to the church. Soon as you can."

She was already sitting up, already reaching for the clothes she had laid out the night before. "What's happened?"

"Fire," James said, and in that single word Ruth heard the collapse of months of rebuilding, the undoing of everything the congregation had poured into restoring Mount Zion after the first arson attack five years earlier. "Started sometime after midnight. By the time neighbors saw the flames, wasn't nothing left to save."

Ruth dressed with the mechanical precision of someone moving through shock, her hands steady even as her heart hammered against her ribs. The second fire in five years felt less like coincidence than like deliberate campaign, a systematic effort to convince Mount Zion Baptist Church that some communities were not welcome to have permanent gathering places.

The drive to the church passed in a blur of familiar streets that now felt strange, as if the landscape itself had been altered by the news of destruction. Ruth found herself thinking of her father, Samuel, who had died three years earlier without seeing his rebuilt church burn a second time. There was mercy in that timing, she realized—mercy in being spared the sight of dreams destroyed twice, hope extinguished repeatedly by the same hatred that refused to let it live.

The lot where Mount Zion had stood was crowded with people despite the early hour, neighbors and congregation members drawn by the same impulse that had brought Ruth—the need to witness destruction, to assess damage, to begin the work of deciding whether to rebuild again or to let this final fire mark the end of their experiment in permanent sanctuary.

The church was gone. Not damaged, not partially destroyed, but completely consumed, leaving only the foundation stones and the old oak tree that had somehow survived both fires like a witness to the congregation's persistence. The smell of smoke still hung in the air, acrid and bitter, carrying the scent of burned hymnals and destroyed dreams.

Ruth walked through the crowd of gathered witnesses, listening to the murmured conversations that mixed grief with anger, despair with determination. Some voices spoke of insurance claims and rebuilding funds, the practical mathematics of restoration.

Others questioned whether Mount Zion was meant to continue, whether two fires in five years constituted a divine message about the wisdom of maintaining such a visible presence in a community where visibility could be dangerous.

Mother Caldwell sat in a folding chair someone had brought from home, her ancient frame wrapped in a quilt despite the morning warmth. At eighty-five, she had survived more destruction than most people could imagine—slavery, Reconstruction, the systematic dismantling of progress, and now the second burning of a church she had helped build twice. Yet her voice carried the same steady faith that had sustained the congregation through decades of smaller defeats.

"Second time somebody tried to burn down our sanctuary," she said to no one in particular and everyone in general. "Second time they succeeded in burning down our building. But they still ain't figured out how to burn down our church."

Ruth knelt beside Mother Caldwell's chair, taking the older woman's weathered hands in her own. "What do you think, Mother Caldwell? Do we rebuild again?"

The question hung in the smoky air like a prayer waiting for answer. Around them, the crowd had grown quiet, understanding that wisdom was being dispensed by someone who had earned the right to speak about persistence in the face of repeated destruction.

"Child," Mother Caldwell said, her voice carrying the particular authority that came from having outlived most of her contemporaries, "I been thinking about that oak tree over there. Been struck by lightning twice, had fire burn all around it twice, seen every kind of storm Carolina weather can throw at it. But look at it—still standing, still giving shade, still growing new leaves every spring."

She paused, letting her gaze move from the tree to the faces of the people gathered around her. "Some things got roots that go deeper than the damage that visits them. Some things got purposes that outlast the people who try to destroy them. Mount Zion Baptist Church is that kind of thing."

The conversation that followed was part grief counseling, part strategic planning, part theological discussion about the relationship between divine will and human determination. Ruth found herself thinking about the lunch counter protest the week before, about the decision to act despite the certainty of consequences, about the way that individual acts of courage accumulated into movements that could not be stopped by arrest or intimidation.

"The people who burned our church," she said, her voice rising above the murmur of smaller conversations, "they think they're burning our hope. They think if they destroy our gathering place enough times, we'll give up and go away. But they don't understand what we're really building here."

The crowd turned toward her with the attention that had become automatic whenever Ruth spoke in public settings. Her reputation as a teacher and civil rights organizer had given her voice particular authority in community discussions, the credibility that came from putting principles into practice even when practice was dangerous.

"We're not just building a place to hold Sunday services," she continued, walking toward the foundation stones that had survived both fires. "We're building a community that refuses to let hatred have the last word. We're building a sanctuary that exists in our hearts and our commitment to each other, not just in wood and brick."

She knelt and placed her hand on one of the foundation stones, feeling the solid reality of what could not be burned, what could not be destroyed by those who mistook buildings for the faith that raised them. "These stones have held through two fires. They'll hold through a third building, and a fourth if necessary, and as many as it takes until the people who keep lighting matches understand that some things can't be destroyed."

The response was not immediate applause but something deeper—the kind of recognition that came when someone articulated what everyone had been feeling but hadn't yet found words to express. One by one, other members of the congregation approached the foundation stones, placing their own hands on the warm granite, making their own silent commitments to the work of rebuilding.

James cleared his throat and stepped forward, his massive frame carrying the authority of someone who had helped lay every stone, drive every nail, raise every wall of both previous church buildings. "If we're going to do this again," he said, "we need to do it right. Not just rebuild the same building and wait for the same people to burn it down. We need to think about what kind of church can survive in a community where some folks would rather see us worship under trees than have a permanent place to call home."

The discussion that followed was practical and visionary in equal measure, the kind of planning that happened when people who had survived repeated destruction refused to let destruction define their possibilities. Someone suggested building with brick instead of wood, fire-resistant materials that would require more than matches to destroy. Someone else proposed a different location, a lot less visible from the main road, less likely to attract the attention of those who saw Black churches as threats to be eliminated.

But Mother Caldwell raised her hand for attention, her gesture carrying enough authority to quiet all the strategic planning and practical considerations. "This lot is where Samuel Washington knelt in the dirt and prayed for a sanctuary," she said. "This is where we buried his hopes in foundation stones and raised his dreams in timber and faith. This is where we're going to keep building until the people who keep burning understand that we're not going anywhere."

Ruth felt something shift in her chest, a movement from grief toward determination that seemed to be shared by the entire crowd. The second fire had been intended to end their story, to convince them that some dreams were too dangerous to pursue, some communities too visible to be allowed to thrive. Instead, it had clarified something essential about who they were and what they were willing to sacrifice to remain who they were.

"Then we rebuild," she said, her voice carrying across the lot with the authority of someone who had already made the decision and was simply informing the world of her intentions. "We rebuild bigger, stronger, and more stubborn than before. We rebuild because our children deserve a sanctuary that can't be burned down by people who are afraid of our prayers."

The crowd stirred with the particular energy that came when individual commitments crystallized into collective determination. This was how movements sustained themselves through repeated defeats—not by avoiding destruction but by proving that their capacity to rebuild was stronger than their enemies' capacity to tear down.

As the morning wore on and the crowd gradually dispersed toward jobs and responsibilities, Ruth remained by the foundation stones, thinking about the distance between the girl who had collected scattered seeds from hostile pavement and the woman who now stood ready to rebuild a church for the third time. The journey had taught her that some acts of faith required repetition, that some dreams demanded the kind of persistence that outlasted the hatred arrayed against them.

The lunch counter protest had been about claiming space that had been denied. The church rebuilding was about the same work on a larger scale—insisting that their community had the right to exist visibly, permanently, and without apology in a world that kept trying to convince them to be grateful for invisible tolerance.

Ruth walked to the old oak tree that had survived both fires, running her hand along bark that bore the scars of repeated trauma but continued to produce new growth each spring. In a few hours she would need to return to her classroom, to the work of teaching children who would inherit whatever world the adults managed to build or rebuild. But first she stood under the oak's shade and offered her own prayer for the work ahead—not a request for easier circumstances but a commitment to match whatever destruction came their way with twice as much determination to build something better in its place.

The morning sun climbed higher, burning away the last traces of smoke and illuminating the foundation stones that waited patiently for the third iteration of Mount Zion Baptist Church to rise from their solid base. Somewhere in the distance, a train whistle called its lonesome song toward destinations unknown. But Ruth was not thinking about distant places. She was thinking about this place, this lot, this community that had decided once again that some dreams were worth rebuilding as many times as necessary until they became impossible to destroy.

Ruth heard it in fragments, each one hitting harder than the last: Dr. King had been shot in Memphis. Dr. King was dead. The whispers and phone calls moved through the Black community faster than newspapers and more accurately than radio broadcasts, carrying the news that would crack the world open. The prophet of nonviolent resistance had been silenced.

by the violence he had spent his life trying to overcome.

Ruth set down the phone in her small kitchen and felt something crack inside her chest—not her heart, which had learned to absorb blow after blow, but something deeper. The framework of hope that had sustained her through lunch counter protests and church burnings, through small victories and crushing defeats, suddenly felt fragile as spun glass in a windstorm.

She had been preparing dinner for her family when the call came, the ordinary Thursday evening routine of a schoolteacher and mother interrupted by news that would divide history into before and after. The pot of greens still simmered on the stove, the cornbread still waited in the oven, but the kitchen felt transformed by the weight of what had been lost, what would never be recovered.

David found her standing at the sink, staring out the window toward the lot where Mount Zion's third incarnation was slowly rising from the foundation stones. Her husband had learned to read the particular stillness that settled over her when the world delivered news too large to process immediately, the way she went quiet when her heart needed time to catch up with her mind.

"Baby?" he said, his voice carrying the gentle concern of someone who understood that the phone call had brought more than ordinary bad news. "What's wrong?"

"They killed Dr. King," she said without turning around, her words falling into the kitchen air like stones into still water. "Shot him in Memphis while he was there supporting the sanitation workers."

David's sharp intake of breath provided the only sound in the suddenly too-quiet kitchen. Through the window, they could both see the church construction site where volunteers would have been working if darkness hadn't ended the day's labor. The partially completed walls looked different now, framed against an evening sky that seemed to mock the idea that building could overcome destruction, that hope could outlast hatred.

"How?" David asked, though they both knew the question was less about mechanics than about meaning, less about the specific details of assassination than about how a world that had produced Dr. King could also produce the people who decided he needed to die.

Ruth turned from the window and looked at her husband with eyes that held twenty years of marriage and ten years of civil rights work, a decade of watching slow progress collide with violent resistance, of believing that love could overcome hatred if enough people were willing to practice love as a discipline rather than just a feeling.

"The same way they always do it," she said, her voice carrying the exhaustion that came from recognizing patterns that should have been broken decades ago. "Wait until he's somewhere helping somebody else, then shoot him down like he's not somebody's father, somebody's husband, somebody's son."

The conversation that followed was less dialogue than shared grief, two people trying to make sense of a loss that felt both personal and cosmic. Dr. King had never visited their small North Carolina town, had probably never heard of Mount Zion Baptist Church, but his death felt like losing a family member, like watching hope itself get gunned down on a motel balcony in Memphis.

Ruth thought about the letter from Birmingham jail that she had read to her students, about the dream speech that had articulated possibilities her heart had been reaching for before she had words to name them. Dr. King had been the voice that made nonviolent resistance sound like more than passive acceptance, that transformed patience from resignation into strategy, that insisted love was not weakness but the most practical force for social change.

"What do we tell the children?" David asked, referring not just to their own kids but to Ruth's students, to the young people in the community who had learned to believe that change was possible because a preacher from Atlanta had proved it could be done without returning violence for violence.

"We tell them the truth," Ruth said, moving to turn off the stove before the greens burned, maintaining the domestic routines that kept life functioning even when larger systems seemed to be collapsing. "We tell them that good people sometimes get killed for being good, and that doesn't mean being good was a mistake."

But even as she spoke the words, Ruth felt doubt creeping into her voice like smoke seeping under a door. The church burnings, the lunch counter arrests, the slow grinding work of changing hearts and laws one person at a time—all of it had been sustained by the belief that nonviolent resistance could actually work, that turning the other cheek was not just moral instruction but practical strategy.

Now the chief advocate of that strategy was dead, killed by someone who had decided that bullets were more effective than ballot boxes, that assassination was more efficient than argument. The murder felt like more than the loss of a leader; it felt like the repudiation of everything he had stood for, the triumph of violence over the patient work of love.

The days that followed Dr. King's assassination blurred together in a haze of grief and anger that seemed to settle over the entire community like fog that refused to lift. Ruth continued to teach, but her lessons felt hollow, her words about progress and possibility mocked by the reality of a world where prophets of peace were gunned down for challenging systems of oppression.

The construction work on Mount Zion continued, but the volunteers worked with less conversation, fewer songs, the kind of grim determination that came when hope had been tempered by repeated exposure to loss. Each board nailed into place, each brick laid in careful courses, felt like acts of defiance against a world that seemed determined to destroy everything they built.

Ruth found herself questioning not just the strategy of nonviolent resistance but the larger project of believing that America could become the country it claimed to be in its founding documents. If they could kill Dr. King, if they could burn churches and bomb Sunday schools and shoot down civil rights leaders with the certainty of impunity, then perhaps the problem was not individual prejudice but systemic corruption, not personal hatred but institutional evil.

The conversation came to a head during a church meeting held in the partially completed sanctuary of the new Mount Zion. The walls were up but the roof was unfinished, leaving the congregation gathered under open sky as they tried to make sense of a loss that felt both personal and historical.

James stood to address the group, his massive frame silhouetted against the evening sky that showed through the absent roof. "Been thinking about Dr. King," he said, his voice carrying the weight of someone who had spent days wrestling with questions that had no easy answers. "Been thinking about whether all this nonviolent resistance was just a way for them to keep us quiet while they figured out better ways to keep us down."

A murmur rippled through the congregation, the sound of people who had been thinking similar thoughts but hadn't yet been willing to voice them in church. The assassination had shaken something fundamental in the civil rights community, raising questions about strategy and tactics that had seemed settled just a week earlier.

"I understand the anger," Ruth said, rising from her place in the makeshift pews that were actually sawhorses with boards laid across them. "I feel it too. But Dr. King didn't preach nonviolence because he thought white people deserved our patience. He preached it because he understood something about the kind of people we wanted to become."

She walked toward the front of the unfinished sanctuary, her footsteps echoing against the exposed beams and bare walls. "Violence might get us some of what we want, but it won't get us the world Dr. King dreamed about. It won't get us the beloved community where children are judged by the content of their character rather than the color of their skin."

Mother Caldwell's voice rose from her chair near the front, carrying the authority of someone who had lived through emancipation, Reconstruction, and decades of systematic attempts to re-enslave people who had tasted freedom. "That man died for believing we could be better than our enemies," she said. "If we let his death turn us into the kind of people who solve problems with bullets, then they killed more than just Dr. King. They killed his dream."

The discussion that followed was heated but respectful, the kind of theological and practical debate that happened when people of faith found their beliefs tested by circumstances that seemed to mock the very idea of faith. Some argued for more aggressive tactics, for meeting violence with violence, for abandoning the moral high ground in favor of more effective strategies. Others insisted that Dr. King's death made nonviolent resistance more necessary, not less, that honoring his memory required continuing his work even when that work seemed impossible.

Ruth listened to the various voices and felt something crystallizing in her own understanding, a recognition that grief and anger could either destroy hope or refine it, could either end the movement or deepen its commitment to principles that transcended immediate circumstances.

"Dr. King is dead," she said when the discussion had reached a natural pause. "But the work he died for is still alive. The children who need better schools are still alive. The families who need decent housing are still alive. The communities that need sanctuary from hatred are still alive."

She gestured toward the unfinished walls that surrounded them, the third iteration of a church that had refused to stay burned down. "This building has been destroyed twice by people who thought they could stop our faith by destroying our gathering place. But we keep rebuilding because we understand that some things are worth building even when they get torn down, worth believing even when belief is dangerous."

The congregation stirred with recognition, understanding that the same principle that had sustained them through repeated church burnings could sustain the larger movement through the assassination of its most visible leader. The work would continue because the work was larger than any individual, more durable than any single life.

As the meeting drew to a close and people began to gather their things, Ruth found herself thinking about the distance between the young woman who had sat at lunch counters demanding equal service and the mother and teacher who now faced the question of how to continue that work in a world where the apostle of nonviolence had been struck down by violence.

The answer, she realized, was the same answer Mount Zion had given to arson: rebuild, stronger and more determined than before. Continue the work not because it was easy or safe, but because it was necessary, because the children watching needed to see adults who refused to let hatred have the final word in conversations about justice and human dignity.

Outside, the evening sky darkened over the construction site where morning would bring another day of building, another day of proving that some dreams were stronger than the violence arrayed against them. Dr. King was dead, but his dream lived on in partially completed churches and unfinished struggles, in the stubborn insistence that love was still more powerful than hatred, even when hatred seemed to be winning all the battles.

Ruth walked home through streets that felt different now, marked by loss but not defined by it. Tomorrow she would return to her classroom, to the work of teaching children who would inherit whatever world the adults managed to build from the rubble of repeated destruction. The lesson would be the same one Mount Zion Baptist Church had been teaching through its own example: some things are worth building over and over again, as many times as necessary, until they become impossible to tear down.

The needle sliding through the fabric made a soft whisper that seemed to carry more weight than the hymns that usually filled Mount Zion's sanctuary. Ruth sat in a circle with twelve other women, their hands busy with the practical work of quilting while their voices wove together the kind of conversation that could only happen when grief had been given time to age into something that looked more like wisdom.

Five years had passed since Dr. King's assassination, but the loss still felt fresh some mornings, like a wound that had healed over but never completely stopped aching. The civil rights movement had continued, evolved, splintered into factions that sometimes seemed to have forgotten they were fighting the same war. But here in the partially completed sanctuary of Mount Zion—still unfinished because funding came in fits and starts, because other crises kept demanding attention—the women continued the quieter work of holding their community together one stitch at a time.

The quilt they were making was intended for the church auction, a fundraiser that had become as much about community building as money raising.

But the pattern Ruth had chosen—a variation on the traditional "Log Cabin" design—carried symbolic weight that none of the women had mentioned directly but all understood. Each block represented a family, a household, a place where people gathered to sustain each other through whatever storms the wider world might bring.

"Pass me that blue thread," Mother Caldwell said, her ancient fingers still nimble despite arthritis that had gnarled her hands into shapes that spoke of decades spent in service to others. At ninety, she was the only person in the circle who remembered slavery firsthand, who could speak from personal experience about the kind of patience required to outlast systems designed to break the spirit.

Ruth handed over the spool and watched Mother Caldwell thread her needle with the practiced efficiency of someone who had been making something beautiful from scraps for most of a century. The blue fabric came from a dress that had belonged to Mrs. Patterson, who had died the previous winter after a life spent cleaning other people's houses and raising other people's children while somehow finding time to grow the gardens that fed half the neighborhood.

"She would have liked being part of this quilt," said Essie Washington, Ruth's mother-in-law, whose steady presence had anchored the church through two fires and countless smaller crises. "Mrs. Patterson always said her happiest times were when she was making something useful with her hands."

The comment opened a space for the kind of remembering that happened naturally when women gathered to work with their hands, when the rhythm of stitching created room for stories that needed telling. Each piece of fabric in the quilt carried history—a shirt that had been worn to important meetings, a dress that had witnessed baptisms and funerals, scraps that had been saved because they were too beautiful to throw away even when the original garments were beyond repair.

Ruth found her own memories drifting back to the early days of the civil rights movement, when the work had seemed more straightforward, when the enemy was more clearly defined, when victory had seemed like something that could be achieved through sufficient courage and determination. The lunch counter protests, the voter registration drives, the marches that had felt like prayers in motion—all of it had been sustained by the belief that America could be shamed into living up to its ideals.

But the years since Dr. King's death had taught harder lessons about the persistence of systems that adapted to resistance, that found new ways to maintain old inequalities. The lunch counters served Black customers now, but housing discrimination kept families trapped in neighborhoods with underfunded schools. Voting rights were protected by federal law, but gerrymandering and poll taxes found creative ways to dilute political power. Progress was real but incomplete, victory partial and always temporary.

"Sometimes I wonder what Dr. King would think about where we are now," Ruth said, her needle pausing in its work as the thought found its way into words. "Whether he'd be proud of how far we've come or disappointed in how far we still have to go."

The question hung in the air like incense, weighty and complex. Some of the women in the circle had heard Dr. King speak in person, had participated in marches where his presence had transformed crowds of individuals into something that felt like the kingdom of heaven breaking into earthly reality. Others knew him only through television and newspapers, but all of them had been shaped by his vision of what America could become if it chose love over fear, justice over convenience.

"Dr. King understood something about change that some folks still haven't figured out," Mother Caldwell said, her voice carrying the particular authority that came from having witnessed multiple generations of struggle. "He knew it wasn't going to happen all at once, like a light switch getting flipped. He knew it was going to be more like sunrise—slow, gradual, with setbacks and shadows, but steady if you kept your eyes on the horizon."

She held up her section of the quilt, examining the stitches with the critical eye of someone who believed that work worth doing was worth doing well. "This quilt's going to take us months to finish, maybe a year. We could rush it, make bigger stitches, get it done faster. But then it wouldn't hold up when somebody needed it to keep them warm. Some things take the time they take because that's what makes them strong enough to last."

Ruth nodded, understanding that the conversation had moved beyond quilting to the larger questions that kept her awake some nights—how to measure progress when change came in increments almost too small to see, how to maintain hope when each victory revealed new layers of work that needed doing.

"Marcus asked me yesterday why we still need to have separate meetings about civil rights," she said, referring to her five-year-old son whose questions had a way of cutting straight to the heart of contradictions adults had learned to live with. "He said if Dr. King already made everything equal, why are we still talking about it?"

The circle of women smiled with the knowing recognition of those who had fielded similar questions from their own children, who had struggled to explain why the world Dr. King dreamed about was still more vision than reality. Children had a way of expecting the promises adults made to be kept on schedule, of assuming that good intentions translated automatically into changed circumstances.

"What did you tell him?" asked Sarah Jenkins, a young mother whose own children were just learning to navigate a world where legal equality existed on paper but practical equality remained elusive in daily experience.

Ruth set down her needle and reached for the thermos of coffee that had become as essential to quilting circles as thread and fabric. "I told him that Dr. King planted seeds, but seeds take time to grow into trees. And some of the ground where the seeds got planted had been hard-packed for so long that it's taking extra time for the roots to break through."

It was the kind of explanation that satisfied children while acknowledging the complexity that adults had to live with—the recognition that changing laws was easier than changing hearts, that dismantling systems was easier than rebuilding communities, that the work of justice was measured not in years but in generations.

The afternoon wore on with the comfortable rhythm of women who had learned to find sanctuary in each other's presence, who understood that some conversations could only happen when hands were busy and voices could drift into the kind of honesty that required time and trust to develop. The quilt grew beneath their fingers, each stitch a small act of faith that the finished product would be stronger and more beautiful than its individual pieces.

As the light began to slant through the unfinished windows of Mount Zion's sanctuary, Ruth found herself thinking about the distance between the angry young woman who had demanded immediate justice at lunch counters and the mother and teacher who now understood that real change happened at the pace of quilts rather than protests, through the accumulated effect of countless small decisions rather than dramatic confrontations.

It wasn't that the fire had gone out of her commitment to civil rights—if anything, becoming a mother had intensified her determination to create a more just world for her children to inherit. But the strategies had evolved, become more patient and more comprehensive, rooted in the understanding that lasting change required not just legal victories but cultural transformation, not just changed policies but changed hearts.

"This quilt's going to outlast all of us," Mother Caldwell said, examining the growing expanse of fabric that had begun to look like something that could actually keep someone warm. "Twenty years from now, some family we've never met is going to wrap themselves in this quilt and feel the love that went into every stitch."

The comment sparked a round of speculation about where the quilt might end up, whose bed it might grace, what stories it might witness. But Ruth found herself thinking less about the quilt's future than about its present function—the way it had created space for the kind of conversation that happened when women gathered to make something useful with their hands, when work and prayer became indistinguishable from each other.

The civil rights movement had been sustained by mass meetings and public demonstrations, but it had been nurtured in spaces like this—kitchens and living rooms and church sanctuaries where people who shared common cause could speak honestly about their fears and hopes, their disappointments and persistent faith that tomorrow could be better than yesterday if enough people were willing to work for it.

"We should put a label on it," Sarah suggested. "Let folks know where it came from, what hands made it."

"Mount Zion Baptist Church Quilting Circle, 1973," Ruth said, imagining the small piece of fabric that would carry their story forward into whatever future awaited the finished quilt. "Made with love by women who believed in building something beautiful from whatever pieces they had to work with."

Edited Text

"Mount Zion Baptist Church Quilting Circle, 1973. Made with love by women who believed in building something beautiful from whatever pieces they had to work with."

As the women began to pack up their supplies...

, stitch them together with whatever tools they had available, and create something that could provide warmth and comfort for people they might never meet but whose lives they hoped to touch through the work of their hands.

As the women began to pack up their supplies and prepare to return to evening routines of cooking and homework supervision, Ruth lingered in the sanctuary, running her hand along the section of quilt she had been working on. The stitches were small and even, the result of techniques her grandmother had taught her on summer afternoons when the world moved at the pace of porch swings and sweet tea.

Tomorrow she would return to her classroom, to the work of teaching children whose questions about justice and equality required answers that acknowledged both how far they had come and how far they still had to go. The lesson would be quilted into her response—that some things take time not because they're not worth doing quickly, but because doing them right required the kind of patience that produced work strong enough to last.

Outside, the evening sky darkened over a community that looked different than it had five years earlier—lunch counters that served everyone, schools that were slowly integrating, voting booths where Black voices joined the conversations that shaped their shared future. The changes were real but incomplete, progress measured in degrees rather than revolutionary transformation.

But inside the partially completed sanctuary of Mount Zion Baptist Church, Ruth folded the finished quilt section and tucked it into her basket. Around her, the other women gathered their thread spools and needles, wrapping scraps in newspaper for next week.

Valley of Dry Bones

Ruth was washing dishes when the news came through the radio. She had the water running, her hands working through the plates mechanically while the evening broadcast played in the background. Then the announcer's voice changed—became urgent, unsteady—and she turned off the faucet to listen.

Dr. Martin Luther King Jr. had been shot in Memphis. He was dead.

The plate slipped from her hands and shattered against the porcelain sink. Ruth stared at the pieces, her hands still suspended in the cold dishwater. The reporter's voice continued, struggling to find adequate words, but she could barely hear it over the roaring in her ears.

She gripped the edge of the counter. The man who had given shape to their hopes, who had taught them that love could be stronger than hatred—gone. Thirty-nine years old. Cut down by a sniper's bullet on an ordinary Tuesday evening.

The grief came first, then the rage, then the grief again, each wave pulling her under before she could catch her breath.

Behind her, the radio continued its litany of details: the Lorraine Motel, the balcony, the single shot that had torn through more than flesh and bone to wound the very heart of the movement. But Ruth had stopped listening to words, could only hear the silence that followed each sentence, the vast emptiness that

Dr. King's death had carved out of the future they had been building together.

David found her there twenty minutes later, still gripping the sink, still staring at the shattered plate as if it contained some explanation for how the world could produce both saints and the people who destroyed them. Her husband's arms wrapped around her from behind, solid and warm, but she could feel his own trembling, could sense that he too was struggling to comprehend a loss that felt both personal and cosmic.

"How do we tell Marcus?" she whispered, referring to their eight-year-old son who had grown up believing that good people like Dr. King always won in the end because God was on their side. The boy had absorbed the mythology of the civil rights movement through bedtime stories and Sunday school lessons, had learned to see the world as a place where righteousness eventually triumphed over evil if enough people were willing to march and pray and refuse to give up.

"We tell him the truth," David said, his voice rough with unshed tears. "That sometimes good people get killed for being good, and that doesn't mean being good was wrong."

But even as he spoke the words, Ruth could hear the uncertainty beneath them, the same questions that were tearing at her own faith. If God was just, how could such injustice persist? If love was stronger than hate, why did hate keep winning the decisive battles? If nonviolent resistance was more than naive idealism, why had its greatest practitioner been gunned down like a common criminal?

The days that followed blurred together in a haze of memorial services and media coverage, of stunned conversations that kept circling back to the same impossible questions. Ruth continued to teach, but her lessons felt hollow, her words about progress and possibility mocked by the reality of a world where prophets of peace were eliminated by people who preferred the certainty of violence to the complexity of change.

Her students, ranging in age from six to sixteen in the consolidated school that served their rural district, looked to her for explanations that she didn't possess, for reassurance that she couldn't honestly provide. How could she tell them that hard work and good character would be rewarded when the man who had embodied both lay dead in Memphis? How could she encourage them to believe in America when America had proven once again that it would rather kill its conscience than listen to it?

The question came to a head during a particularly difficult afternoon when her youngest students asked why Dr. King had to die. Ruth stood before the classroom, looking into faces that still held the innocence she was being asked to help shatter, and felt the weight of responsibility that came with being the adult who had to explain evil to children who deserved a world without it.

"Sometimes," she said carefully, choosing words that would convey truth without destroying hope, "there are people who are afraid of change, even good change. Dr. King wanted to change things so that all of God's children would be treated fairly, and some people were so afraid of that change that they thought the only way to stop it was to hurt Dr. King."

A small hand shot up from the second row. "But didn't God protect him? I thought God protected good people."

Ruth felt something crack in her chest, the sound of certainties breaking under pressure they were never meant to bear. The theology that had sustained her through lunch counter protests and church burnings, through voter registration drives and countless smaller acts of courage, suddenly seemed as fragile as the plate she had dropped in her kitchen sink.

"God did protect Dr. King," she said finally, the words coming from some deep place that she hadn't known still existed. "God protected the important part—his message, his dream, his love. Those things can't be killed with bullets. They live on in people like us who remember what he taught and keep trying to make his dream come true."

It was the kind of answer that satisfied eight-year-olds while acknowledging the complexity that adults had to live with—the recognition that divine protection operated according to different mathematics than human safety, that sometimes the most protected life was the one that gave itself completely to a cause larger than individual survival.

But walking home through the April evening that still carried winter's chill, Ruth found herself questioning not just her ability to comfort children but her own capacity to continue believing in the vision Dr. King had articulated. The beloved community he had preached about seemed impossibly distant in a world where beloved leaders were assassinated for the crime of loving too inclusively, too dangerously, too hopefully.

The conversation she had been avoiding came that night after Marcus was asleep and she and David sat in their small living room, surrounded by the accumulated artifacts of a life built on the assumption that tomorrow would be better than today. The bookshelves held volumes by Dr. King and Gandhi, by Thoreau and Jesus, by all the voices that had convinced them that nonviolent resistance was not just morally superior but practically effective.

"I keep thinking about Birmingham," Ruth said, breaking a silence that had stretched through most of the evening. "About how proud we felt reading his letter from jail, how sure we were that he was showing us the way forward. Now I wonder if we were just naive, if we confused moral clarity with political strategy."

David looked up from the newspaper he had been pretending to read, his eyes reflecting the same doubt that had been eating at Ruth since the assassination. "You think he was wrong? About nonviolence, about love conquering hate?"

"I don't know what I think anymore," Ruth admitted, the words feeling like confession and blasphemy combined. "I know that every advance we've made, they've found ways to roll back. Integration led to white flight. Voting rights led to gerrymandering. Fair housing laws led to redlining with different names. And now they've killed the one person who could hold the movement together, who could keep us focused on love instead of revenge."

The admission hung in the air between them like smoke from a fire that wouldn't quite go out. For fifteen years, their marriage had been sustained by shared commitment to the vision Dr. King had articulated—the belief that America could become the country it claimed to be in its founding documents if enough people were willing to work for it with sufficient patience and determination.

Now that vision seemed as distant as the stars, beautiful and inspiring but ultimately unreachable by people whose feet were planted firmly on earth, whose children needed more than dreams to protect them from the violence that seemed to be the only language America understood when confronted with demands for justice.

"Maybe the problem isn't with Dr. King's vision," David said slowly, as if testing each word before speaking it. "Maybe the problem is that we expected too much too fast. Maybe love does conquer hate, but it takes longer than we thought, costs more than we were prepared to pay."

Ruth wanted to believe him, wanted to find comfort in the possibility that Dr. King's death was not the repudiation of everything he had stood for but simply the price of prophetic witness in a world that had always killed its prophets. But the comfort felt thin against the weight of grief that had settled over her like a lead blanket, heavy with the accumulated disappointment of watching too many good people pay too high a price for believing that goodness could change the world.

The weeks that followed Dr. King's assassination brought riots to Washington and Baltimore, flames that seemed to consume not just buildings but the mythology of peaceful protest that had sustained the civil rights movement through its most difficult years. Ruth watched the news coverage with a mixture of horror and understanding, recognizing in the burning cities the same rage that had been building in her own chest—the accumulated fury of people who had tried patience and received bullets in return.

Her own students reflected the confusion that seemed to have settled over the entire Black community like fog that refused to lift. Some spoke with new admiration for Black Power advocates who had always argued that white America would only respond to force. Others clung more desperately to Dr. King's teachings, as if embracing nonviolence more completely could somehow resurrect their fallen leader. Most simply seemed lost, caught between grief and anger with no clear path forward.

The crisis came to a head during a particularly heated discussion in her classroom when one of her older students asked why they should continue to follow Dr. King's example when following his example had gotten him killed. The question carried the sharp edge of adolescent logic that had not yet learned to soften truth with diplomacy, but it voiced what many adults were thinking but were afraid to say aloud.

"Because," Ruth said, surprising herself with the firmness in her voice, "Dr. King didn't preach nonviolence because he thought white people deserved our patience. He preached it because he knew that violence would turn us into the kind of people we were fighting against, would make us part of the problem instead of part of the solution."

She walked to the window that looked out over the schoolyard where children played games that seemed to mock the adult world's capacity for destroying beautiful things. "Dr. King understood that how we fight determines what we become. If we fight with hatred, we become hateful. If we fight with violence, we become violent. If we fight with love, we become loving, even if love gets us killed."

The student who had asked the original question raised his hand again. "But Miss Ruth, if love gets us killed, how does it help anybody? Dead people can't change anything."

Ruth felt the question pierce through the comfortable abstractions of theology to the practical reality of parents who wanted their children to survive more than they wanted them to be martyrs. The same question that had kept her awake too many nights since the assassination, the same doubt that had made her wonder if she was raising Marcus to be noble or naive.

"Dr. King isn't dead," she said, the words coming from some deep place that she hadn't known was still intact. "His body is gone, but everything important about him is still alive. His words are still alive. His dream is still alive. His love is still alive in everyone who refuses to let hatred have the last word."

She turned back to face the classroom, seeing in their young faces the same mixture of hope and skepticism that she had been wrestling with since that terrible Tuesday evening. "Violence might get us some of what we want, but it won't get us the world Dr. King dreamed about. It won't get us the beloved community where all of God's children can live together as brothers and sisters."

The discussion that followed was more mature than Ruth had expected from students so young, touching on questions of strategy and morality that many adults were afraid to examine too closely. Some argued that Dr. King's death proved the futility of nonviolent resistance. Others insisted that his assassination made continuing his work more necessary, not less.

But Ruth found herself thinking less about the tactical arguments than about the spiritual ones, less about what worked than about what was right, what honored the best impulses of the human spirit rather than the worst. The lunch counter protests and voter registration drives had been sustained not just by the hope of changing laws but by the conviction that they were engaged in the work of becoming fully human, of refusing to let oppression diminish their capacity for love.

That afternoon, as the school emptied and Ruth sat alone in her classroom grading papers, she found herself returning to one of Dr. King's sermons that she had read so many times she could recite passages from memory. It was the one about loving your enemies, about returning good for evil, about the revolutionary power of redemptive love.

The words seemed impossibly idealistic in a world that had just proved once again that it preferred to kill love rather than be transformed by it. But they also carried a stubborn truth that even assassination couldn't destroy—the recognition that some responses to evil actually multiplied evil, while others had the mysterious power to transform it into something that served life rather than death.

Ruth closed her grade book and walked to the window, watching the late afternoon sun slant across the schoolyard where tomorrow her students would return with their questions about justice and love, about whether good people always lost and bad people always won. She didn't have perfect answers for them—Dr. King's death had shattered too many of her certainties for easy comfort.

But she had something more valuable than answers: she had the stubborn conviction that the questions themselves mattered, that raising children who cared about justice was worth the risk of raising children who might be disappointed by the world's failure to deliver justice on schedule. She had the accumulated wisdom of a community that had survived slavery and Reconstruction and decades of systematic oppression by refusing to let external circumstances determine their internal response to life.

Most importantly, she had the example of Dr. King himself—not the mythologized version that would emerge in later years, but the flesh-and-blood man who had chosen love even when love was dangerous, who had preached hope even when hope seemed naive, who had died believing that the universe bent toward justice even when justice seemed impossibly distant.

Walking home through streets that felt different now, marked by loss but not defined by it, Ruth found herself humming one of the spirituals that had sustained her people through centuries of struggle. The melody was minor key, acknowledging the reality of suffering, but it resolved into major, insisting that suffering did not have the final word in the conversation between hope and despair.

Tomorrow she would return to her classroom, to the work of teaching children who would inherit whatever world the adults managed to salvage from the wreckage of repeated disappointment. The lesson would be the same one Dr. King had been teaching when the bullet found him—that love was stronger than hate not because it always won the immediate battles, but because it was the only force that could win the war for the human soul without destroying what made victory worth having in the first place.

The evening sky darkened over a community that looked the same as it had before the assassination but felt fundamentally altered, like a familiar song played in a different key. Change would continue, but it would happen at the pace of human hearts rather than human laws, through the accumulated effect of countless daily decisions to choose love over fear, hope over cynicism, construction over destruction.

In the distance, the partially completed walls of Mount Zion Baptist Church stood silhouetted against the stars, still unfinished after years of construction but growing steadily stronger with each passing season. The church had survived two fires and would survive this assassination, not because it was protected from destruction but because it was rooted in something deeper than any individual life, more durable than any single death.

Ruth turned the key in her front door and stepped into the warmth of home, where her husband and son waited with questions she couldn't fully answer and love she could completely trust. Outside, the work of justice continued at its own necessary pace—slower than martyrs deserved, faster than oppressors preferred, steady as the faith that refused to let even Dr. King's death mark the end of the dream he had died trying to make real.

The morning brought news that settled over the community like ash from a distant fire. Ruth heard it first through the network of whispers and phone calls that carried urgent information faster than newspapers: the textile mill was closing, moving operations to Mexico where labor was cheaper and regulations were fewer. Three hundred jobs would disappear by Christmas, taking with them the economic foundation that had sustained Black families in their town for two generations.

She set down the phone and felt the familiar weight of crisis settling on her shoulders—not the sharp shock of Dr. King's assassination, which had been sudden and overwhelming, but the grinding pressure of economic reality that moved slowly and inexorably, crushing hope under the weight of market forces that operated according to mathematics that made no allowance for human need.

The mill closure would ripple through the community like stones thrown into still water, each circle of impact growing wider and more devastating. The workers who lost their jobs directly would be only the beginning. The local businesses that depended on their patronage would follow. The tax base that funded schools and public services would shrink. The young people who might have stayed in town to raise their families would leave for cities that offered better prospects, taking with them the energy and optimism that kept small communities alive.

Ruth thought about her students, about the ones whose parents worked at the mill, whose college dreams had been built on the foundation of steady paychecks that would no longer exist. She thought about the families who had scrimp and saved to buy homes they might now lose, who had invested their hopes in a future that corporate executives in distant offices had decided was no longer profitable enough to sustain.

It was a different kind of violence than Dr. King's assassination, but violence nonetheless—the systematic destruction of communities in the name of economic efficiency, the sacrifice of human dignity on the altar of profit margins, the casual cruelty of systems that treated people as disposable inputs in calculations that valued money more than lives.

The community meeting was held that evening in Mount Zion's fellowship hall, the church having finally been completed the previous year with funds raised through fish fries and bake sales, revival services and the stubborn determination of people who refused to let their sanctuary remain unfinished indefinitely. The room was packed beyond capacity, folding chairs arranged in tight rows that still couldn't accommodate everyone who had come seeking answers to questions that had no easy solutions.

Pastor Williams, who had succeeded Ruth's father as Mount Zion's spiritual leader, opened the meeting with a prayer that asked for wisdom and strength rather than miracles—the kind of prayer that acknowledged God's sovereignty while recognizing human responsibility for the practical work of survival. His voice carried the weight of someone who had presided over too many funerals for young men destroyed by unemployment, too many families torn apart by economic desperation.

The mill supervisor who had been sent to explain the closure spoke with the practiced tone of someone who had delivered similar news in other towns, his words carrying the bland efficiency of corporate communications that had been scrubbed clean of any acknowledgment of human cost. The decision was final, he explained. Global competition made the closure inevitable. Severance packages would be modest but fair. The company regretted any inconvenience.

Ruth listened from her seat near the back and felt rage building in her chest like steam in a pressure cooker. Inconvenience. As if three hundred families losing their livelihoods was comparable to a delayed flight or a broken appliance. As if generations of workers who had given their labor and loyalty to the company were merely statistics in a spreadsheet that balanced more favorably without them.

When the supervisor finished his presentation and opened the floor for questions, the room erupted with the accumulated anger of people who had been treated as expendable. Voices overlapped in a chorus of frustration and desperation: What about the pensions we were promised? What about the health insurance for families with sick children? What about the town that had given tax breaks and infrastructure improvements to attract the mill in the first place?

The answers were what everyone had expected—legal obligations would be met, but nothing more. The company had shareholders to consider, competitors to match, profit margins to maintain. The human costs of closure were unfortunate but unavoidable consequences of operating in a global economy that showed no mercy to sentiment or tradition.

Ruth found herself thinking about the distance between this meeting and the civil rights gatherings of her youth, between the clear moral lines of segregation and the complex economic realities that were destroying communities without the courtesy of declaring their racial motivations. The mill closure would devastate Black and white families equally, would leave children of all colors wondering why their parents had lost jobs through no fault of their own.

It was harder to organize resistance when the enemy was market forces rather than individual prejudice, when the solution required changing global economic systems rather than local laws. How do you march against unemployment? How do you sit in at a factory that was moving to another country? How do you love your enemies when your enemies were abstract forces that had no faces, no consciences, no capacity to be shamed into better behavior?

After the supervisor left, escorted by security guards who had been hired in anticipation of community anger, the meeting continued with the practical work of figuring out how to survive collective catastrophe. Ideas flew like sparks from a fire—cooperative businesses that could provide alternative employment, political organizing to attract new industries, educational programs that could retrain workers for different kinds of jobs.

But Ruth could hear the desperation beneath the brainstorming, the recognition that three hundred good jobs couldn't be replaced by wishful thinking and community gardens. The economic foundation that had supported middle-class Black life in their town was crumbling, and no amount of determination could rebuild it without resources that seemed impossibly out of reach.

The conversation was interrupted by a commotion near the front of the room, where someone's wife had collapsed from what looked like a combination of exhaustion and despair. Ruth pushed through the crowd to help, her teacher's training kicking in automatically when crisis demanded practical response. The woman was conscious but shaking, overwhelmed by the prospect of losing everything she and her husband had worked decades to build.

"What are we going to tell the children?" the woman whispered as Ruth knelt beside her chair. "How do you explain to a ten-year-old that Daddy lost his job not because he did anything wrong, but because some people in New York decided they could make more money somewhere else?"

Ruth felt the question pierce through her own professional composure to the place where her deepest fears lived—the recognition that the world her son was inheriting was in some ways more dangerous than the one she had grown up in, because the enemies were harder to identify and the solutions less clear. Legal segregation had been evil, but it was evil with a human face that could be confronted and eventually shamed into retreat. Economic oppression operated through systems that seemed as impersonal as weather, as inevitable as gravity.

"The same way we've always told them hard truths," Ruth said, helping the woman sit up and accept a cup of water from one of the church mothers. "We tell them that sometimes life is unfair, but that doesn't mean we stop fighting for fairness. We tell them that sometimes people make decisions that hurt other people, but that doesn't mean we become people who hurt others. We tell them that their worth doesn't depend on having a job, and their future doesn't depend on what happens to one factory in one town."

It was the kind of answer that comforted children while acknowledging the complexity that adults had to live with, the recognition that resilience was less about avoiding hardship than about refusing to let hardship define the limits of possibility. But speaking the words to someone else's child made Ruth acutely aware of how difficult they would be to apply to her own family if David lost his job at the mill, if their modest middle-class life evaporated along with the economic foundation that had made it possible.

The meeting eventually wound down with the formation of committees and task forces, with exchange of phone numbers and promises to stay in touch, with the practical arrangements that communities made when faced with collective crisis. But Ruth could sense that something fundamental had shifted in the room, a recognition that the strategies that had worked against legal segregation were inadequate against economic forces that operated according to different rules, that respected no boundaries except profit margins.

Walking home through streets that looked the same but felt different, Ruth found herself thinking about the sermons her father used to preach about the valley of dry bones, about Ezekiel's vision of resurrection in the midst of apparent death. Samuel Washington had applied those scriptures to the civil rights movement, had taught his congregation to see their struggles as part of God's larger plan to bring justice to the world.

But what did resurrection look like when the thing that had died was not individual hope but collective economic opportunity? How did you prophesy life into situations where market forces had decreed death? How did you maintain faith in divine justice when global capitalism seemed more powerful than any god most people were willing to worship?

The questions followed Ruth into her house, where David sat at the kitchen table with papers spread before him—resume drafts, job applications, the practical detritus of a man trying to figure out how to reinvent himself at forty-five. He looked up as she entered, his face drawn and hollow. Hours of confronting the reality that skills honed over decades might be worthless in an economy that valued mobility over loyalty, flexibility over expertise—it had worn him down to something she barely recognized.

"How was the meeting?" he asked, though his tone suggested he already knew the answer.

"About what we expected," Ruth said, settling into her chair and accepting the cup of coffee he poured from the pot that had been keeping warm since supper. "Company's not changing their mind, government's not stepping in to save us, and we're on our own to figure out what comes next."

They sat in the comfortable silence of a marriage that had learned to absorb crisis without being destroyed by it, that had survived the assassination of heroes and the burning of churches and countless smaller disappointments by refusing to let external circumstances determine their internal response to life. But this felt different, more fundamental, like watching the ground itself shift beneath their feet.

"I keep thinking about Marcus," David said finally. "About what kind of world we're leaving him, what kind of future he's going to have if this is what happens to communities that try to build something stable."

Ruth looked through the kitchen window toward the house across the street, where the Johnsons lived with their three children, all of whom were in her classes, all of whom would be affected by the mill closure in ways that hadn't fully become clear yet. Tomorrow she would face a classroom full of students whose questions about the future would require answers that acknowledged both the reality of economic hardship and the possibility that hardship didn't have to define the limits of human possibility.

"Maybe that's the lesson," she said, surprising herself with the steadiness in her voice. "Maybe we teach him that building something stable doesn't mean building something that can't be destroyed. Maybe we teach him that stability comes from knowing who you are and what you believe, not from having a job or a house or any of the things that can be taken away."

It was a hard lesson to accept, much less teach—the recognition that security was less about external circumstances than internal resources, that the only things that couldn't be destroyed were the things that lived in human hearts rather than human institutions. But it was also the lesson that had sustained her people through slavery and Reconstruction and decades of systematic oppression, the understanding that survival required roots deeper than economics, stronger than any system designed to extract profit from human labor.

The conversation continued past midnight, touching on practical concerns and philosophical questions, on immediate needs and long-term hopes. By the time they finally went to bed, Ruth and David had reached no definitive answers about their family's future, but they had reached something more valuable—a renewed commitment to face whatever came with the same stubborn grace that had carried them through previous crises.

Outside, the night sky stretched over a community that looked the same but was fundamentally different, marked by loss but not defined by it. The mill closure would bring hardship, would force families to make choices they had never wanted to make, would change the trajectory of lives that had been built on the assumption of steady work and predictable futures.

But it would not destroy the things that mattered most—the bonds between neighbors who had learned to depend on each other, the faith that had sustained them through previous valleys of dry bones, the stubborn insistence that human dignity was not determined by employment status or economic circumstances. Those things were built into the foundation of who they were as a people, and no corporate decision made in distant boardrooms could demolish what had been constructed by generations of survival and mutual aid.

Ruth fell asleep thinking not about what they were losing but about what remained, about the classroom full of students who would still need teaching, about the community that would still need the kind of love that built up rather than tore down. Tomorrow would bring new challenges and old questions, but it would also bring new opportunities to prove that some things were stronger than market forces, more durable than economic systems, as persistent as hope itself.

The letter arrived on a Thursday morning in November, carried by a mail carrier who had no idea he was delivering the collapse of a dream twenty years in the making. Ruth recognized the official letterhead of the county school board before she opened the envelope, knew from the weight of the paper and the formality of the address that this was not routine correspondence about curriculum or supply orders.

Due to declining enrollment and budgetary constraints resulting from recent industrial closures, the Board of Education regrets to inform you that your position will be eliminated at the end of the current academic year. Your years of dedicated service to our students are deeply appreciated...

The words blurred together as Ruth read them, her mind struggling to process what felt like a physical blow rather than mere information. Twenty-three years of teaching, two decades of investing herself in the minds and hearts of children who had grown up to become nurses and mechanics, soldiers and parents, contributing members of society who carried pieces of what she had given them into their own lives and work.

Now the school board had decided that her contribution was no longer financially viable, that the mill closure had reduced enrollment to levels that couldn't justify maintaining her position. She was being eliminated, like a line item in a budget that no longer balanced, like an expense that had outlived its usefulness to people who measured education in cost per pupil rather than impact per life.

Ruth set the letter on the kitchen table and stared at it as if prolonged examination might reveal some alternative interpretation, some hidden clause that would transform termination into temporary reassignment. But the words remained stubbornly clear, bureaucratically precise, final as death and just as irreversible.

The teaching job had been more than employment for Ruth—it had been calling, identity, the practical expression of her belief that education was the most effective form of civil rights work. Every child she had taught to read was a victory against ignorance. Every student she had encouraged to dream beyond their circumstances was a blow struck against systems designed to limit human potential based on zip code and skin color.

Now that work was ending, not because she had failed at it but because the economic foundation that made it possible had been pulled out from under the entire community like a rug yanked away by unseen hands. The mill closure had started a cascade of consequences that was still gathering momentum, destroying not just individual jobs but the collective infrastructure of opportunity that had sustained middle-class Black life in their town.

Ruth walked through the house that she and David had bought fifteen years earlier, when teaching salaries and mill wages had made homeownership possible, when the future had seemed secure enough to justify thirty-year mortgages and college savings accounts. The living room walls were covered with photographs from her classroom—graduation ceremonies and award presentations, field trips and holiday parties, the visual record of a career spent believing that investing in children was investing in the future.

Now that future seemed as uncertain as morning fog, likely to evaporate as soon as harsh reality arrived in the form of unemployment benefits that would last only so long, savings accounts that were modest to begin with, and a job market that had few openings for teachers approaching fifty who were considered too expensive by younger administrators looking to balance budgets on the backs of experience.

The phone rang, interrupting her inventory of loss and limitation. The voice belonged to Sarah Jenkins, a fellow teacher who had received her own elimination notice that morning, who was calling to share the misery and confusion that came with having a life's work declared surplus to requirements.

"Twenty-six years," Sarah said, her voice tight with tears that had been flowing since she opened her own letter. "Twenty-six years of perfect attendance, of staying late to help struggling students, of spending my own money on supplies because the district couldn't afford what the children needed. And they eliminated my position with a form letter that probably went out to a dozen other teachers."

Ruth listened to her friend's pain and felt her own anger crystallizing into something harder and more focused than grief. The school board members who had voted to eliminate their positions had never spent eighteen-hour days preparing lessons and grading papers. They had never stayed after school to counsel children whose home lives were chaos, never used their own grocery money to buy snacks for students who came to class hungry because there was no food at home.

"What are you going to do?" Ruth asked, though she already knew the answer would echo her own uncertainty.

"I don't know," Sarah admitted. "My husband's job at the mill is already gone. Our savings won't last more than a few months if we're both unemployed. I'm fifty-two years old—who's going to hire a teacher my age when they can get someone fresh out of college for half the salary?"

The conversation continued for another twenty minutes, touching on practical concerns and emotional devastation in equal measure. Both women had built their adult identities around the work of teaching, had found meaning and purpose in the classroom that extended far beyond paychecks and benefits. Now they faced not just unemployment but the loss of the roles that had defined them, that had given structure and significance to their daily lives.

After hanging up, Ruth found herself drawn to the cardboard boxes she had brought home to begin the process of packing up her classroom—twenty-three years of accumulated materials that represented thousands of hours spent preparing lessons, creating bulletin boards, collecting resources that might someday prove useful for helping children learn. The prospect of sorting through it all felt overwhelming, like being asked to dismantle her own professional identity one textbook at a time.

The work would have to wait, though, because she had more immediate concerns in the form of students who were still showing up to her classroom every day, still needing the education that the county had decided was no longer financially sustainable. Ruth had made a commitment to finish the year strong, to ensure that her final months of teaching were worthy of the two decades that had preceded them.

But walking into school the next morning felt different, like entering a building that was already haunted by its own future abandonment. The hallways echoed with the knowledge that several teachers would not be returning, that programs were being eliminated, that the comprehensive education that had served the community for generations was being reduced to whatever bare minimum the reduced budget could support.

Ruth's students sensed the change even before official announcements were made. Children had a way of picking up on adult anxiety, of understanding through intuition that something important was ending even when no one explained exactly what was being lost. Their questions became more pointed, their attention more focused, as if they understood that time was running out for learning whatever their teacher had left to give them.

"Miss Ruth," asked one of her sixth-graders during afternoon reading time, "is it true that some teachers aren't coming back next year?"

Ruth looked around the classroom at faces that reflected her own investment in their future, at children she had taught not just to read and write but to think critically about the world they were inheriting, to believe that education was the key to opportunities that might otherwise be denied them. How could she explain that their community had been deemed economically unviable, that their education was being sacrificed to balance budgets that had been unbalanced by decisions made in boardrooms they would never see?

"Some changes are coming," she said carefully, choosing words that would convey truth without destroying hope. "But what won't change is your ability to learn, to grow, to become whatever you choose to become. That doesn't depend on having a particular teacher in a particular building. That depends on what's inside you, on your determination to keep learning no matter what obstacles you face."

It was the kind of answer that satisfied children while acknowledging the complexity that adults had to live with, the recognition that resilience was less about maintaining ideal circumstances than about adapting to whatever circumstances actually existed. But speaking the words made Ruth acutely aware of how much easier it was to preach adaptability than to practice it, how much more difficult it was to remain hopeful when your own future had been declared surplus to requirements.

The afternoon brought another piece of difficult news in the form of a phone call from Marcus, now fifteen and old enough to understand the economic pressures that were reshaping his world. He had heard about the teacher layoffs from classmates whose parents worked for the school district, had connected his mother's situation to his own uncertain future in ways that demonstrated the sharp intelligence she had spent years nurturing.

"Mom," he said without preamble when she answered the phone, "are we going to have to move? Are you and Dad both going to be unemployed at the same time?"

Ruth felt the question pierce through her professional composure to the place where her deepest fears lived as a mother, the recognition that the economic forces destroying her community were also threatening her son's stability, his sense of security, his ability to finish high school in the place where he had started it. The boy who had once asked innocent questions about why Dr. King had to die was now old enough to understand that sometimes entire ways of life could be eliminated by people who never had to live with the consequences of their decisions.

"We're going to figure it out," she said, surprised by the steadiness in her own voice. "That's what families do—we figure out how to take care of each other no matter what changes come our way. Your father and I have been through difficult times before, and we've always found a way to make things work."

But even as she spoke the reassuring words, Ruth could hear the uncertainty beneath them, the recognition that this crisis felt different from the civil rights struggles of her youth because the enemy was harder to identify and the solutions less clear. You could organize against segregated lunch counters, but how did you organize against global economic forces that treated entire communities as expendable? How did you fight back against systems that operated according to mathematical logic that made no allowance for human cost?

After Marcus hung up, Ruth remained at her desk in the empty classroom, surrounded by the familiar artifacts of her teaching career—student artwork covering bulletin boards, class photos spanning two decades, the accumulated evidence of thousands of small victories in the daily work of education. Tomorrow she would continue preparing lessons for students who still needed teaching, would maintain the routines and expectations that made learning possible even in the midst of institutional collapse.

But tonight she sat alone in the gathering darkness, thinking about the distance between the young civil rights activist who had believed that changing laws could change the world and the middle-aged teacher who was learning that some battles required different strategies, longer timelines, deeper reserves of faith than she had imagined possible.

The letter of termination lay in her purse like a small weight, a reminder that twenty-three years of service could be eliminated with bureaucratic efficiency that would have impressed the segregationists she had once fought against. But it could not eliminate what she had learned about resilience in those years, what she had discovered about the capacity of human beings to adapt and survive and continue growing even when the institutions that had sustained them crumbled around them.

Outside, the November evening settled over a community that was learning to grieve not just individual losses but the death of entire ways of life, the end of assumptions about stability and progress that had sustained middle-class dreams for generations. But inside the classroom where Ruth had spent her career planting seeds that would outlast any particular school or district, the work continued at its own necessary pace—slower than politicians promised, faster than despair expected, steady as the faith that refused to let economic hardship have the final word in conversations about human possibility.

The sound that woke Ruth at two in the morning was not quite crying, not quite moaning, but something between the two—the kind of sound that emerged from grief too deep for ordinary expression. She found David in Marcus's room, standing beside their son's bed in the darkness, his shoulders shaking with sobs that seemed to come from some place deeper than disappointment, more fundamental than fear.

Marcus slept on, unaware that his father was watching him with the particular desperation of a man who had built his identity around providing for his family and now faced the prospect of having nothing left to provide except his presence, his love, his stubborn determination to continue being a father even when fatherhood could no longer be measured in paychecks and college savings accounts.

Ruth slipped her arm around David's waist and felt him lean into her embrace, accepting comfort that couldn't solve their practical problems but could make them bearable for another day, another week, another season of uncertainty that stretched ahead like winter without promise of spring. They stood together in their son's room, listening to the quiet breathing of a boy who still trusted that his parents could protect him from a world that seemed determined to disappoint everyone who believed in the possibility of security.

"I don't know how to do this," David whispered, his words carrying the weight of a man who had worked at the same job for twenty-two years, who had defined himself through steady employment and reliable income, who now faced the prospect of reinventing himself at an age when most people expected their careers to be settled rather than starting over.

"You do it the same way we've done everything else," Ruth whispered back, her words carrying the accumulated wisdom of a marriage that had survived the assassination of heroes and the burning of churches, that had learned to find stability in each other rather than in external circumstances. "One day at a time, trusting that we'll find what we need when we need it."

It was easy to say and harder to believe, but belief was less important than practice in the work of surviving collective crisis. Tomorrow would bring more questions without easy answers, more challenges that required improvisation rather than expertise. But it would also bring the opportunity to prove once again that some things were stronger than economic systems, more durable than employment status, as persistent as love itself.

They returned to their own bedroom and lay awake in the darkness, holding hands across the space between their pillows, listening to the familiar sounds of a house that might not be their home much longer if unemployment stretched beyond their modest savings. But for now it was still theirs, still filled with the accumulated memories of fifteen years spent believing that hard work and good character would be rewarded with stability and security.

The belief had proven naive, but the work and character remained—qualities that could not be eliminated by corporate decisions or school board votes, that belonged to them regardless of employment status or economic circumstances. Ruth fell asleep thinking not about what they were losing but about what remained, about the classroom full of students who still needed teaching, about the family that still needed holding together, about the community that still needed the kind of love that built up rather than tore down.

Morning would come with its own demands and possibilities, but for now there was only the quiet darkness and the sound of breathing that marked the rhythm of survival, the stubborn insistence of life continuing even when the structures that had sustained it were crumbling all around. Some things endured not because they were protected from destruction but because they were rooted in something deeper than any system designed to extract profit from human hope, stronger than any force that measured worth in dollars rather than dignity.

The valley of dry bones stretched out before them, littered with the remains of dreams and institutions that had seemed permanent just months before. But somewhere in that valley, new life was stirring—not the resurrection of what had been lost, but the birth of what might still become possible when people refused to let destruction have the final word in conversations about their own worth, their own future, their own stubborn determination to keep building something beautiful from whatever pieces remained.

Learning to Lament

The sound that filled Mount Zion's sanctuary on Sunday mornings had changed—not the voices themselves, but what they carried. Hope had aged into something closer to endurance than expectation. Ruth stood before the small choir, her hands raised to guide voices that knew instinctively how to find harmony in the spaces between joy and sorrow, between the promises of Scripture and the reality of empty pews where families displaced by economic collapse used to sit.

She had become the church's music director almost by accident, stepping into the role when the previous director moved north to find work after the mill closure. What had begun as a temporary arrangement had evolved into something that felt like calling—the discovery that she could channel her own grief and frustration into musical arrangements that gave voice to what the congregation was feeling but couldn't always articulate in prayer or conversation.

The hymn she had selected for this morning was "Precious Lord," but not the version most people knew. Ruth had arranged it to begin in minor key, acknowledging the valley they were walking through, before gradually modulating to major—not as denial of their circumstances but as insistence that sorrow and hope could coexist in the same heart, the same song, the same faith that had carried them through slavery and segregation and now this peculiar form of economic exile that left communities intact but emptied of purpose.

"Take my hand, precious Lord, lead me on," the voices sang, and Ruth could hear in the harmonies the accumulated wisdom of people who had learned that being led by God did not guarantee easy paths, only the promise that no path would be walked alone. Mrs. Henderson's alto carried the weight of a woman who had lost her husband to a heart attack three months after he lost his job. Young Timothy's tenor reflected the determination of a recent high school graduate who had decided to stay in town and help his grandmother rather than leave for college like most of his classmates.

The song finished in a silence that was fuller than applause, thick with recognition that music could sometimes say what preaching could not, could offer comfort that came not from answers but from the simple acknowledgment that questions themselves were worthy of beautiful expression. Ruth lowered her hands and looked out over the congregation—smaller than it had been five years ago, grayer, marked by loss but not defined by it.

Pastor Williams rose to deliver his sermon, but Ruth's attention was drawn to the back of the sanctuary, where she noticed a figure that hadn't been there when service began. A young woman, maybe twenty-five, very still. She'd come seeking something she couldn't name, who had found her way to this place through whatever combination of desperation and hope led people to push open church doors when they had nowhere else to turn.

The woman was clearly struggling—not just economically, though her clothes suggested that money was tight, but with something deeper. There was a hollowness around her eyes that Ruth recognized from her own mirror during the darkest days after losing her teaching position, the look of someone who had invested their identity in external circumstances and discovered that external circumstances were less reliable than morning fog.

After the service, during the informal fellowship time that had become one of Mount Zion's most important ministries, Ruth made her way toward the visitor. The woman was standing apart from the small clusters of conversation, close enough to observe but far enough to escape if social interaction proved too overwhelming for whatever internal crisis had brought her there.

"I'm Ruth Johnson," she said, offering her hand with the careful warmth she had learned to extend to people who might interpret kindness as intrusion. "Welcome to Mount Zion. I don't think we've met."

The woman's hand trembled as they shook. "I'm Angela," she said, her voice rough. "Angela Davis. I just... I heard the singing from outside and thought maybe..."

She let the sentence trail off, but Ruth understood. Churches served many functions in communities like theirs, but perhaps the most important was providing sanctuary for people who needed a place to be broken without judgment, to sit in the presence of others who understood that faith and despair were not opposites but often uncomfortable roommates in the same human heart.

"The music has been helping me too," Ruth said, choosing her words to create space for honesty rather than demanding it. "Sometimes I think we need songs for the valleys as much as we need songs for the mountaintops. Maybe more."

Angela's eyes brightened. Someone understood. Spiritual maturity sometimes meant learning to lament beautifully rather than always demanding reasons to celebrate.

"I used to sing," Angela said, the words coming out like a confession. "In college, before... before everything fell apart. I thought maybe I could be a music teacher, work with children, make a difference. But then I couldn't find a job, and my student loans were more than I could handle, and my father got sick, and I had to move back home to take care of him..."

Ruth listened to the familiar litany of dreams deferred by circumstances beyond individual control, the story that had become common in their community as economic opportunities disappeared faster than the people who depended on them. Angela's narrative was different in its specifics but identical in its essential structure—the collision between aspiration and reality, between what seemed possible and what actually proved sustainable.

"Would you like to join our choir?" Ruth asked, the invitation emerging from instinct rather than calculation. The choir could always use another voice, but more than that, Angela looked like someone who needed to add her voice to others, to discover that individual pain could become collective beauty.

Angela's response was immediate tears—not the bitter tears of frustration but the softer tears of relief, the moisture that came when unexpected grace arrived in forms simple enough to accept. "I... I don't know if I remember how. It's been so long since I sang anything except lullabies to my father when he couldn't sleep."

"Lullabies are good training," Ruth said, understanding that the woman before her had been doing musical ministry without recognizing it, had been offering comfort through song even when her own comfort was in short supply. "The best church music comes from people who know something about needing to be comforted."

The conversation was interrupted by Mother Caldwell, who approached with the careful steps of someone whose body had outlasted its warranty but whose spirit remained stubbornly engaged with the world around her. At ninety-three, she was the acknowledged keeper of institutional memory, the living link between Mount Zion's founding generation and its uncertain future.

"I heard this young lady mention she could sing," Mother Caldwell said, her voice carrying the authority of someone who had spent nine decades learning to discern character through close observation. "We been praying for the Lord to send us some help with the music ministry. Seems like prayers sometimes get answered in ways we don't expect."

Angela looked between Ruth and Mother Caldwell with the expression of someone who had grown accustomed to doors closing but wasn't quite sure how to respond when one opened. "I'm not sure I'm ready for... I mean, my life is pretty complicated right now. I'm not sure I have much to offer anybody else."

"Child," Mother Caldwell said, settling into a nearby pew with the deliberate movements of extreme age gracefully managed, "you think any of us got our lives figured out? You think we standing here singing about trusting the Lord because everything's going smooth for us?"

She gestured toward the sanctuary that surrounded them, the building that had been destroyed twice by arson and rebuilt three times through the stubborn determination of people who refused to let hatred have the final word in conversations about where they were allowed to worship.

"This church been teaching people to sing in the storm for fifty years. We got expertise in making beautiful music out of broken circumstances. What we don't got is enough voices to carry all the songs our hearts need to sing."

The simplicity of the invitation cut through Angela's defenses like warm light through cold morning air. Here was a community that not only acknowledged brokenness but had learned to transform it into something that served life rather than death, hope rather than despair. Here were people who understood that sanctuary was not about perfection but about the willingness to show up with whatever fragments you could contribute to the collective work of healing.

"When do you practice?" Angela asked, her voice gaining strength as the possibility of belonging began to feel real rather than theoretical.

"Wednesday nights, seven o'clock," Ruth replied. "But we also gather informally sometimes when someone needs to work through a particularly difficult song, or when the regular Sunday hymns aren't quite capturing what we need to express."

It was an invitation to more than musical participation—it was an offer to join the ongoing conversation between faith and doubt that sustained communities through their darkest seasons, to add her voice to the ancient work of transforming individual suffering into collective strength.

Angela accepted with a nod that carried more weight than words, understanding that she was agreeing to more than choir practice. She was choosing to believe that her broken places could contribute to something beautiful, that her voice mattered even when it carried the roughness of too much crying, too many disappointments, too many nights of singing lullabies to a dying father who deserved better than he had received from a world that measured worth in economic productivity.

As the fellowship time continued and the sanctuary gradually emptied, Ruth found herself thinking about the distance between the civil rights activist of her youth and the music director of her middle age. The work looked different now—less dramatic, more patient, focused on sustainability rather than breakthrough. But it was still the work of justice, still the insistence that all of God's children deserved dignity and belonging and the opportunity to contribute their gifts to something larger than their individual circumstances.

The evening found Ruth at her kitchen table, preparing music for Wednesday's choir practice and thinking about how to incorporate Angela's voice into arrangements that had been crafted for the voices they already had. It was the kind of practical problem that had become metaphor for larger challenges—how to make room for new people in communities that had learned to survive by maintaining tight bonds among existing members, how to remain open to growth when growth required energy that was already stretched thin by the work of simple survival.

David joined her at the table, carrying the cup of tea that had become their nightly ritual since unemployment had eliminated the structure that work schedules used to provide their evenings. They had developed new routines to replace the old ones, new rhythms that acknowledged their changed circumstances without being defined by them.

"How was church?" he asked, settling into his chair with the careful movements of a man whose body had been shaped by two decades of mill work and was still learning to adapt to the absence of physical labor.

"We got a new choir member," Ruth said, looking up from the sheet music she had been arranging. "Young woman named Angela, been taking care of her dying father, looks like she's about at the end of her rope. But she's got music in her, and she's looking for a place to let it out."

David nodded with the understanding of someone who had learned to recognize the signs of people in crisis, who had seen enough neighbors struggle through job loss and family illness and the various forms of heartbreak that seemed to accumulate when economic foundation crumbled beneath entire communities.

"Music seems to be helping folks more than preaching these days," he observed, referring to the way the congregation responded differently to hymns than to sermons, as if melody could reach places that words alone couldn't touch.

"Music's always been how we learned to tell the truth about difficult things," Ruth replied, thinking about the spirituals that had sustained enslaved people, the freedom songs that had powered the civil rights movement, the hymns that had helped previous generations navigate their own valleys of dry bones.

"Maybe that's what we need right now—not answers, but better ways to ask the questions that don't have easy answers. Better ways to hold hope and grief in the same heart without pretending one of them isn't real."

The conversation drifted into comfortable silence, each of them absorbed in their own work—David with the job applications that had become his daily discipline despite the scarcity of opportunities, Ruth with the musical arrangements that had become her way of processing not just her own loss but the collective grief of a community learning to sing its way through circumstances that no one had been prepared to face.

Outside, the October evening settled over streets that looked the same but felt different, marked by the absence of shift changes and factory whistles, by the presence of too many people who should have been working but instead were learning to fill days that no longer had the structure of employment to give them shape and meaning.

But inside houses where people gathered around kitchen tables to work on whatever problems they could solve, the ancient work continued—the work of figuring out how to maintain dignity when external circumstances seemed designed to strip it away, how to preserve hope when hope required more faith than seemed reasonable to expect from finite human beings.

Ruth finished arranging the harmony parts for "Precious Lord" and set the music aside, satisfied that she had created space for

Angela's voice without disrupting the balance that the existing choir members had learned to maintain. Tomorrow she would begin the work of teaching the new arrangement, of helping individual voices learn to blend into something larger than themselves, more beautiful than any single voice could produce alone.

It was, she realized, the same work she had been doing in various forms her entire adult life—helping people discover that their individual gifts mattered most when they were offered in service of something beyond individual need, that the most powerful form of resistance to systems designed to isolate and diminish people was the simple act of joining voices in songs that insisted on the possibility of harmony despite evidence to the contrary.

The work would continue tomorrow, and the day after that, and for as many days as it took for voices to learn new songs, for broken hearts to discover that brokenness could be transformed into beauty if enough people were willing to sing together in the key of stubborn hope.

The crack epidemic arrived like a flood, sudden and devastating, transforming familiar streets into landscapes of desperation that no one had been prepared to navigate. Ruth first noticed it in her students—the ones whose attendance became erratic, whose attention wandered to places no child should have to visit, whose small bodies carried the weight of adult worries about parents who disappeared for days at a time, about utilities getting cut off, about evictions that came without warning when drug addiction consumed whatever money had been set aside for rent.

The mill closure had created the conditions—too many people with too much time and too little hope, too many young men who had expected to follow their fathers into steady work but instead found themselves watching their parents' generation struggle with unemployment that felt less like temporary setback than permanent exile from the American dream. Into that vacuum had come dealers who understood that despair was a market opportunity, that addiction was a growth industry that thrived in communities where legitimate economy had collapsed.

Ruth saw the effects every day in her remaining part-time teaching position—the one the school board had offered her after budget cuts eliminated her full-time job, a consolation prize that paid a fraction of her former salary but at least kept her connected to the children who needed what she had to offer more desperately than ever. The classroom had become a refuge for students whose home lives had been destabilized by parents' addiction, whose basic needs for food and safety and adult attention were no longer being met by families too consumed by chemical escape to provide care for anyone else.

But it was the funeral of Deacon Thompson's son that brought the crisis fully into focus, that forced the community to confront what had been happening in individual households as a collective tragedy requiring collective response. Michael Thompson had been twenty-eight years old, a young man who had grown up in Mount Zion's Sunday school, who had sung in the youth choir, who had graduated high school with plans to attend technical college before the economic collapse eliminated both the college program and the job prospects that would have made education worthwhile.

Ruth arrived at the church early to help prepare music for the service, but found herself instead standing in the fellowship hall with other women from the congregation, looking at a young man's body that bore the unmistakable signs of overdose—that stillness when life departs suddenly, violently. The sight hit her hard, not just because death was always shocking but because this death felt preventable in ways that made grief inseparable from rage.

"He was trying to get clean," Mrs. Thompson told the women who had come to sit with her before the service began. Her voice carried the exhaustion of a mother who had spent two years watching her son cycle through periods of sobriety and relapse, who had learned to hope cautiously and grieve repeatedly as addiction claimed pieces of the boy she had raised until finally claiming all of him.

"Had been clean for three months, longest stretch in two years. Got a job at the gas station, was talking about maybe taking some classes at the community college. Then something happened—I don't know what—and he disappeared for a week. When they found him..."

She couldn't finish the sentence, but didn't need to. Everyone present understood the mechanics of overdose, the way that tolerance worked, how people who had been clean for weeks or months could kill themselves with amounts of drugs that had once been routine. They understood because Michael was not the first young person they had buried in the past year, was not the only family in their congregation learning to navigate grief complicated by shame and anger and the terrible knowledge that love had not been enough to save someone who deserved saving.

Ruth listened to Mrs. Thompson's story and felt familiar anger rising in her chest—not just at the dealers who had sold poison disguised as relief, but at the systems that had created the conditions where poison felt like the only available relief. The young men turning to drugs were not inherently different from the young men who had once expected mill jobs and middle-class stability. They were the same people, facing different circumstances, responding to despair with whatever tools their environment provided.

The service itself was unlike any funeral Ruth had experienced at Mount Zion. Usually, homegoing services were celebrations of lives well-lived, opportunities to give thanks for years of faithful service and Christian witness. But Michael's death required a different kind of liturgy, one that could acknowledge the waste and tragedy of addiction while still affirming the worth of a life that had been cut short by forces larger than individual moral failure.

Pastor Williams preached from the valley of dry bones, speaking about resurrection and renewal, about God's ability to breathe life into situations that appeared beyond hope. But Ruth could see in the faces of the congregation that the usual comfort was not quite reaching the places where comfort was most needed. How do you preach resurrection to parents burying children who died not from accident or illness but from the systematic destruction of opportunity that had left entire communities vulnerable to predators who trafficked in chemical despair?

It was during the musical portion of the service that something shifted, when Angela stepped forward to sing a solo that Ruth had arranged specifically for the occasion. The song was "Trouble Don't Last Always," but Angela's arrangement transformed it from a simple assertion of faith into something more complex—a lament that acknowledged the reality of trouble while insisting that acknowledgment was not the same as acceptance.

Angela's voice had developed strength and range in the months since joining Mount Zion's choir, but more than technical skill, it had gained the kind of emotional authority that came from personal experience with the troubles she was singing about. Her father had died six months earlier, not from overdose but from the kind of despair that consumed him gradually, leaving her to navigate grief and survivor's guilt and the practical challenges of rebuilding a life that had been organized around caregiving.

As she sang, Ruth could see the congregation responding not just to the music but to the recognition that here was someone who understood their pain from the inside, who was not offering false comfort but authentic witness to the possibility that pain could be transformed into something that served life rather than death. The tears that flowed were not just for Michael but for all the young people who had been lost to addiction, for all the families learning to carry grief that felt too heavy for human shoulders.

After the service, during the meal that followed in Mount Zion's fellowship hall, Ruth found herself in conversation with a group of women who were grappling with the same questions that had been keeping her awake at night. How do you maintain faith in divine justice when injustice seemed to be winning all the visible battles? How do you continue to invest in community when community was being systematically destroyed by forces that operated beyond local control?

"I keep thinking about what we could have done differently," said Mrs. Jenkins, whose own son had been arrested the previous month for possession, who was facing the choice between mortgage payments and legal fees. "Whether there were signs we missed, conversations we should have had, ways we could have protected our children from something we didn't even see coming."

Ruth understood the impulse toward self-blame, the way that parents especially wanted to believe that love and vigilance could have prevented tragedies that were actually the predictable result of policy decisions made in places far from their influence. But she also understood that accepting responsibility for systemic problems was a form of false comfort, a way of maintaining the illusion of control in situations where control had been systematically removed from communities like theirs.

"The problem isn't that we failed our children," she said, her words carrying the authority of someone who had spent decades working with young people, who had seen too many bright futures destroyed by circumstances beyond individual control. "The problem is that our children are growing up in a world that failed them first—that eliminated their economic opportunities, that criminalized their communities, that offered them drugs when it should have offered them jobs."

The conversation that followed was more political than spiritual, touching on questions of policy and power that churches usually avoided but could no longer ignore when the effects were sitting in their fellowship halls, buried in their cemeteries, locked up in their county jails. The crack epidemic was not a natural disaster but a man-made catastrophe, the result of specific decisions about drug policy, economic development, criminal justice that had been made without regard for their impact on communities that lacked political power to protect themselves.

But even as they analyzed the systemic roots of their crisis, the women around the table kept returning to more immediate concerns—how to support families dealing with addiction, how to create alternatives for young people who saw drug dealing as their only economic opportunity, how to maintain hope in a community where too many funerals were becoming routine rather than shocking.

"We need to start a support group," suggested Mrs. Patterson's daughter, who had moved back to town after college to help care for her aging mother and found herself confronting a community that looked nothing like the one she had left five years earlier. "Not just for the addicts, but for their families. People who are trying to love someone through addiction without enabling them, who are trying to figure out the difference between helping and hurting."

Ruth nodded, understanding that support groups were a form of ministry that churches were uniquely positioned to provide—safe spaces where people could speak honestly about their struggles without fear of judgment, where the ancient work of bearing one another's burdens could take practical form in contemporary crisis.

"And we need to think about prevention," added Angela, who had joined the conversation after finishing her cleanup duties in the sanctuary. "Programs for kids who haven't started using yet, alternatives that give them something to hope for, something to work toward that doesn't involve selling drugs or buying drugs or any of the other ways people are trying to survive when survival feels impossible."

The ideas that emerged from their conversation were modest in scope but ambitious in vision—after-school programs that would provide safe spaces for children whose parents were struggling with addiction, job training initiatives that could prepare young adults for whatever employment opportunities did exist, community gardens that could provide both food security and meaningful work for people who needed structure and purpose in their daily lives.

None of it would solve the larger problems that had created the conditions for epidemic addiction, but all of it represented the kind of local response that communities could organize when national and state governments proved unwilling or unable to address crises that were devastating entire regions. It was the same impulse that had built Mount Zion Baptist Church from foundation stones and community determination—the refusal to wait for outside rescue when internal resources could be mobilized for mutual aid and collective survival.

As the evening wound down and people began to head home to their own grief and their own plans for continuing the work that Michael Thompson's death had clarified, Ruth found herself thinking about the distance between the civil rights movement of her youth and the community organizing that her middle age was demanding. The enemies were less visible now, harder to march against, but the work remained essentially the same—creating conditions where all of God's children could thrive rather than merely survive, could contribute their gifts to something larger than their individual circumstances.

Walking through streets that looked the same but felt different, marked by the absence of people who should have been there and the presence of people who shouldn't have needed to be there, Ruth felt the familiar weight of work that was larger than any individual's capacity but essential enough to demand whatever energy she had available to give.

Tomorrow would bring new challenges and old questions, but it would also bring new opportunities to prove that love was stronger than addiction, hope more durable than despair, community more powerful than the forces that sought to destroy it one person at a time. The work would continue because the work was necessary, because children deserved better than what they were inheriting, because people like Michael Thompson deserved to be remembered not just as cautionary tales but as beloved children of God whose lives had been cut short by systems that could be changed if enough people were willing to work for change.

The night sky stretched over a community that was learning to grieve collectively without being paralyzed by grief, to face crisis without being defined by it, to maintain faith not in easy answers but in the slow, patient work of building something better from whatever pieces remained after destruction had done its worst. It was hard work, holy work, the kind of work that had sustained communities through slavery and segregation and now this particular form of economic and social warfare that targeted the most vulnerable with precision that would have impressed military strategists.

But it was also the work that Ruth had been training for her entire adult life, through teaching and civil rights organizing and music ministry and all the other forms that love took when it was practiced as discipline rather than sentiment, when it was offered as service to something larger than individual comfort or security. The work would continue, and she would be part of it, for as long as her voice could contribute to the choir of people who refused to let destruction have the final word in conversations about human possibility.

The phone rang before dawn. Ruth answered on the second ring, already knowing. "Ruth, honey, you need to come," Mrs. Henderson said, her voice rough with tears and exhaustion through long nights when death took its time arriving. "Miss Essie... she's asking for you. Doctor says it won't be much longer."

Ruth was already moving toward the closet, already pulling on clothes with the automatic efficiency of someone who had learned to respond quickly to medical emergencies, family crises, the urgent needs of a community where everyone was connected by bonds deeper than blood. Essie Washington, her mother-in-law, had been declining for weeks, her ninety-two-year-old body finally succumbing to the accumulation of years and work and heartbreak that had been held at bay by will power and community need for longer than medical science could explain.

The drive to the house where David had grown up, where Essie had raised four children on a domestic worker's wages and a faith that could move mountains when mountains needed moving, passed in a blur of familiar streets that felt strange in the early morning light. Ruth found herself thinking not about death but about legacy, not about what was ending but about what would continue, what would be passed down through the generations of people who had been shaped by Essie's particular combination of toughness and tenderness.

The house was full when Ruth arrived, filled not just with family but with the extended network of neighbors and church members and children grown to adulthood who had found in Essie Washington a source of wisdom and comfort that their own circumstances had failed to provide. The front room had been transformed into something between hospital and sanctuary, the bed positioned where Essie could see visitors, where conversations could flow around her even when she lacked strength to participate actively.

Ruth approached the bedside and took Essie's hand, feeling the bones that had grown fragile as bird wings, the skin that had become translucent with age but still carried the warmth of a woman who had spent nine decades learning to love people through their worst moments as well as their best. Essie's eyes opened at the touch, focusing with effort on Ruth's face, registering recognition that carried the weight of twenty-five years of shared family life.

"Ruth, baby," Essie whispered, her voice barely audible but clear in its intention. "You been taking good care of my boy. Taking good care of that grandbaby. I can rest easy knowing that."

The words carried more weight than their simplicity suggested, containing within them the accumulated approval of a woman whose opinion had shaped family decisions for decades, whose blessing had been sought on matters ranging from career choices to child-rearing philosophy. Ruth felt tears starting in her eyes, not just for the impending loss but for the recognition that she was being entrusted with carrying forward something precious and irreplaceable.

"Miss Essie," she said, her voice thick with emotion that had been building since the first phone call, "you taught me how to be a Johnson, how to be part of this family. I don't know how to do it without you."

Essie's hand tightened around Ruth's with strength that seemed to come from some source deeper than physical reserves, the way that dying people sometimes found energy for final conversations that needed to happen before release became possible. "You already know how, child. You been doing it for twenty-five years. You been loving that man when loving was hard, raising that boy to know who he is and where he comes from, keeping this family together through all kinds of storms."

The conversation was interrupted by David's arrival from the kitchen, where he had been making coffee for the stream of visitors who would continue arriving throughout the day, who would want to pay their respects to a woman whose influence had extended far beyond her immediate family to touch the lives of anyone who had needed mothering in a community where mothers often had to work too many hours to mother their own children as much as they wanted to.

Ruth moved to make room for David beside his mother's bed, watching as his composed adult facade cracked to reveal the boy who had never stopped needing his mother's approval, her guidance, her particular way of loving that made no allowances for weakness but infinite allowances for human frailty. The relationship between them had always been complicated—the tension between a son who wanted to protect his mother from hardship and a mother who had learned that protection was less important than preparation for whatever hardships could not be avoided.

"Mama," David said, taking Essie's other hand, "is there anything you need? Anything we can do to make you more comfortable?"

Essie smiled with effort, the expression transforming her face from mask of pain into something that resembled the woman who had raised him, who had sent him off to his first day of school with pressed shirts and packed lunches and the kind of confidence that came from being loved completely despite imperfect circumstances.

"I need you to take care of each other," she said, her words including not just David and Ruth but the larger family network that extended throughout the house and beyond, the community of people who had learned to function as extended family because biological families alone were not large enough to provide all the support that survival required.

"I need you to remember what your daddy taught about building things that last, about laying foundation that can hold whatever gets built on top of it. I need you to keep building, keep hoping, keep believing that tomorrow can be better than today if enough people are willing to work for it."

It was the closest thing to a final sermon that Essie would offer, the distillation of ninety-two years of wisdom into practical instruction for the people who would have to continue living after she was gone. Ruth listened to the words and felt them settling into her heart like seeds planted in prepared ground, like promises that would need time and tending to fully understand their implications.

The day continued with the rhythm of deathbed vigils—conversations that started and stopped according to Essie's energy, visitors who came to offer final respects or simply to sit in the presence of someone who had shaped their understanding of what it meant to live with dignity in circumstances that seemed designed to strip dignity away. The house filled and emptied and filled again, a constant flow of people who needed to be present for an ending that was also a beginning, a death that would release Essie from suffering while releasing her influence into the care of everyone who had learned something essential from her example.

It was during the afternoon, when the house had grown quiet except for the immediate family, that Essie asked Ruth to sing. Not a hymn or spiritual, but a lullaby—the same song that Ruth had sung to Marcus when he was small, that Essie had sung to David and his siblings, that had been passed down through generations of mothers who understood that music could provide comfort when words were insufficient.

Ruth's voice was rough with emotion and exhaustion, but she sang anyway, letting the simple melody carry whatever love and gratitude she couldn't express through ordinary conversation. The lullaby seemed to ease something in Essie's breathing, to provide the kind of peace that medical intervention could not touch, the comfort that came from being surrounded by voices that had learned to harmonize over decades of shared experience.

As evening approached and the light began to fade from the windows, Essie's breathing grew more labored, her periods of consciousness shorter and less coherent. But her hand remained warm in Ruth's, her presence still substantial enough to anchor the gathering of people who had come to witness her transition from life to whatever came after life, from the woman they had known to the memory they would carry forward.

She died as the sun was setting, as the house filled with the particular quiet that comes when breathing stops and the work of a lifetime reaches its completion. Ruth felt the moment like a physical sensation, a lightness that entered the room as Essie's spirit departed, leaving behind the shell of a body that had carried her through nine decades of joy and sorrow, triumph and disappointment, love offered and love received in the endless circulation of human connection.

The silence that followed was not empty but full—thick with memories and gratitude, with grief and relief mixed together in proportions that would take time to sort out. Ruth continued holding the hand that no longer held back, unwilling to break the connection that had sustained their relationship even when physical strength was no longer available to maintain it.

David's voice broke the silence with a prayer that was more thanksgiving than petition, acknowledging God's grace in allowing them to have Essie for as long as they did, asking for strength to honor her memory through the way they chose to live the lives she had helped shape. It was the kind of prayer that transformed farewell into commissioning, that recognized death as graduation rather than failure.

The hours that followed were filled with the practical work of death—phone calls to funeral homes and insurance companies, arrangements for services that would need to accommodate the dozens of people who would want to pay their respects, decisions about flowers and music and all the details that allowed communities to mark the passing of someone whose life had mattered in ways that extended far beyond family boundaries.

But Ruth found herself thinking less about funeral arrangements than about legacy arrangements, about how to preserve and pass forward the wisdom that Essie had embodied, the particular way of loving that had sustained families through decades of uncertainty and hardship. How do you teach children to have the kind of faith that builds churches and raises families and maintains hope through circumstances that seemed designed to destroy hope?

The answer, she realized, was the same way Essie had taught it—through daily example, through the accumulation of small acts of love and service that demonstrated what values looked like when they were practiced rather than merely preached. Through the patient work of showing young people that dignity was not dependent on external circumstances, that worth was not measured by economic productivity, that community was something you built with your own hands rather than something you waited for others to provide.

The funeral service three days later filled Mount Zion's sanctuary beyond capacity, the church that Essie had helped build through her own labor and financial sacrifice, the sanctuary that had survived fires and neglect and economic collapse because people like Essie Washington had refused to let it die. Pastor Williams preached from the Book of Proverbs, about virtuous women whose worth was far above rubies, whose children rose up and called them blessed.

But it was the music that truly captured Essie's legacy—songs arranged by Ruth and sung by a choir that included Angela and several other voices that had been drawn to Mount Zion by the welcome it offered—sanctuary from storms they couldn't weather alone.

The spirituals and hymns that filled the sanctuary were the same ones Essie had sung while hanging laundry on lines behind houses where she cleaned for families who never learned her children's names, the same melodies she had hummed while cooking meals that stretched to feed whoever showed up hungry at her table.

Ruth stood before the choir, her hands guiding voices that knew instinctively how to transform individual grief into collective celebration, personal loss into community affirmation of all that could not be lost when a life like Essie's reached its earthly completion. The music became prayer and testimony combined, acknowledgment of sorrow that was also insistence on joy, recognition of ending that was also commitment to continuation.

After the service, as the congregation gathered in the fellowship hall for the meal that followed all Mount Zion homegoings, Ruth found herself in conversation with young mothers who had brought their children to pay respects to a woman who had helped raise half the community, who had provided guidance and comfort to anyone who needed mothering beyond what their own circumstances could provide.

"How did she do it?" asked one of the younger women, holding a toddler who had fallen asleep against her shoulder during the long service. "Raise four children on domestic wages, help build a church, take care of half the neighborhood, and still have energy left over to love everybody who needed loving?"

Ruth looked around the fellowship hall at the evidence of Essie's influence—children grown to adulthood who still spoke of her as the mother who had taught them to read, elderly neighbors who credited her with getting them through periods of illness or unemployment, families whose own mothers had worked too far from home to provide the daily guidance that Essie had offered freely to anyone who needed it.

"She understood something about time that I'm still learning," Ruth said, thinking about the way Essie had moved through her days with deliberate attention to each person who crossed her path, each task that required her hands, each opportunity to plant seeds of kindness that might grow into something beautiful decades later.

"She knew that loving people was not something you did in your spare time, after all the important work was finished. She knew that loving people was the important work, that everything else was just what you did to support the real work of building community one relationship at a time."

It was a hard lesson to accept in a world that measured productivity in dollars and efficiency in speed, that treated human connection as luxury rather than necessity. But it was also the lesson that had sustained communities like theirs through slavery and segregation and now this peculiar form of economic exile that left people intact but emptied of the structures that had once provided purpose and direction.

As the afternoon wore on and the crowd began to thin, Ruth found herself alone in the sanctuary for a few minutes, looking at the space where Essie's casket had rested just hours before. The flowers were still there, arrangements sent by families Essie had helped, organizations she had served, the beauty shop where she had gotten her hair done every Saturday for thirty years, the bank where she had made deposits from envelopes that contained coins saved from grocery money and dollar bills earned by ironing other people's clothes.

David joined her in the quiet sanctuary, his arm settling around her shoulders with the automatic comfort of twenty-five years of marriage, of shared grief and shared determination to honor the woman who had taught them both how to love each other through circumstances that tested the limits of human endurance.

"She was ready," he said, his voice carrying the mixture of sadness and peace that came from watching someone die well, surrounded by love and confident in the legacy they were leaving behind. "At the end, when it was just family, she said she could see Daddy waiting for her. Said the church looked different from where she was going—bigger, brighter, full of all the people who had helped build it."

Ruth leaned into her husband's embrace and felt the weight of inheritance settling on her shoulders—not material inheritance, though Essie had left them the house and a small savings account, but the spiritual inheritance that came with being entrusted to carry forward the work that Essie could no longer do herself. The work of loving people through their worst moments, of maintaining hope when hope required more faith than seemed humanly possible, of building community from whatever materials were available when conventional resources proved inadequate.

"I keep thinking about Marcus," Ruth said, referring to their fifteen-year-old son who had grown up with Essie's constant presence, who had learned from her the same lessons about dignity and service that had shaped his father's character. "About what we're supposed to teach him about how to live, how to love people, how to keep building when everything around you seems to be falling apart."

"We teach him the same way she taught us," David replied. "By showing him what it looks like to choose love over fear, service over comfort, hope over the easier mathematics of despair. By letting him see us make the same choices she made, every day, in situations that don't feel heroic but add up to heroism over time."

The conversation was interrupted by Angela, who approached with the hesitation of someone still learning her place in the extended family network that Mount Zion provided for people whose biological families couldn't meet all their needs for connection and support. In the months since joining the choir, she had become not just a singer but a student of how communities like theirs worked—the informal systems of mutual aid and support that operated alongside official institutions.

"Miss Ruth," she said, her voice carrying the respect that younger community members offered to women like Ruth and Essie, who had earned authority through decades of service rather than formal appointment, "I wanted to thank you for letting me be part of today, for including me in something so important.

Miss Essie... she made me feel welcome here when I didn't think I had anything to offer anybody."

Ruth smiled at the recognition that Essie's influence was already continuing through the people she had touched, the way that kindness offered to one person rippled outward to affect people who had never met the original source but benefited from its ongoing effects. Angela's transformation from broken young woman to contributing community member was part of Essie's legacy, evidence that the work of loving people into wholeness continued even after the person who started it was no longer available to see the results.

"Miss Essie would have said that you always had something to offer," Ruth replied. "She would have said that people don't need to have their lives figured out before they can contribute to community. She would have said that sometimes the people who have been broken are the best at helping other people put their pieces back together."

As the evening settled over Mount Zion and the sanctuary gradually emptied, Ruth remained for a few minutes more, thinking about the distance between the young civil rights activist who had demanded immediate justice and the middle-aged church mother who was learning that the most important victories happened slowly, quietly, in individual hearts rather than public demonstrations.

Essie's death marked the end of an era in Ruth's own life—the transition from being someone's daughter-in-law to being the matriarch, from learning the traditions to being responsible for passing them forward, from receiving wisdom to being expected to dispense it to the next generation of people who would need guidance through their own storms and sorrows.

It was a daunting inheritance, but also a precious one—the opportunity to continue work that had sustained communities through centuries of hardship, that had proven more durable than any system designed to destroy the bonds between people who had learned to depend on each other for survival and hope in equal measure.

Walking home through streets that felt different now, marked by absence but not emptied of presence, Ruth found herself humming the lullaby she had sung at Essie's bedside, the melody that had been passed down through generations of women who understood that some things were too important to be left to chance, too precious to be entrusted to institutions that might disappear when budgets tightened or priorities shifted.

The song would continue, carried forward by voices that had learned it from voices stretching back to women who had sung their children to sleep in slave cabins and freedom shacks and company houses and government projects, through all the iterations of hardship that had tested but never broken the determination to raise children who knew they were loved, valued, capable of building something better from whatever materials they inherited from previous generations.

Tomorrow would bring new challenges and old questions, but it would also bring new opportunities to practice the lessons that Essie Washington had spent ninety-two years teaching—that love was stronger than fear, hope more durable than hardship, community more powerful than any force that sought to divide and diminish the human capacity for caring about something larger than individual comfort or security.

The work would continue, and Ruth would be part of it, for as long as her voice could contribute to the choir of people who refused to let death have the final word in conversations about legacy, who insisted that some things lived on in the hearts and hands of everyone who had been touched by their example, transformed by their love, commissioned by their memory to keep building something beautiful in a world that seemed determined to tear beautiful things down.

Prodigal's Return

The afternoon sun, now thin and gold, slanted through the stained-glass windows of Mount Zion, falling across the empty pews. Ruth sat at the piano, her fingers resting silently on the keys. The weekly choir practice had ended an hour ago, but she had stayed, drawn by the quiet. A call from Marcus, fresh and full of the crisp energy of his Atlanta life, still echoed in her mind.

Her gaze drifted over the sanctuary. It felt larger these days, the pews emptier than she ever remembered from her childhood. The faint scent of dust and old wood was more noticeable now, a reminder of a building aging alongside its congregation. The vibrant energy of the civil rights years had given way to a quieter, more stubborn endurance. The mill was a silent monument on the edge of town, and with it had gone so many of the young families, scattering like the seeds she had once tossed onto hard ground, hoping for a harvest.

Marcus had been full of news—a new high-rise project, the possibility of partnership at his firm. She was proud, a deep and honest pride that warmed her chest. He had achieved everything they had prayed for, everything her father Samuel had dreamed of for his descendants: a life of opportunity, free from the limitations they had fought so hard to dismantle.

But beneath the pride was a quiet, persistent ache. His world was one of glass and steel, of metrics and market forces. He knew how to build, but she worried he was forgetting *what for*. Samuel had built a sanctuary to hold a community's hope. She wondered what, exactly, her son's beautiful buildings were built to hold. He spoke of gentrifying neighborhoods and luxury condominiums, and her heart tightened with the memory of families displaced, of communities hollowed out by the very progress he was helping to create.

Her eyes fell to the hymnal open on the piano. She turned a page, her fingers tracing the title of an old spiritual about finding one's way home. She hadn't chosen it for the choir—it was too somber for a Sunday morning—but it was the song her heart needed to sing. With a soft sigh, she began to play, the melody a quiet lament that filled the empty church. It was a prayer not for Marcus's success, but for his memory—that he would remember the foundation stones beneath his feet, and that one day, the path he was on would lead him back not just to Durham, but to the man she had raised him to be.

The morning light streamed through the floor-to-ceiling windows of Marcus's corner office, thirty floors above Atlanta's glittering sprawl. He stood before a scale model of the Riverwalk Gateway, a sleek waterfront development of glass and steel that promised to redefine the city's skyline. It was his masterpiece, the project that would make him senior partner before his thirty-sixth birthday.

"The residential tower maximizes the river view," Marcus explained, his voice confident as he addressed the developers. "While the tiered retail space creates a natural pedestrian flow from the street, inviting the city in." He moved a piece of the model, demonstrating a point. "It's not just a building; it's a destination."

The lead developer nodded, impressed. "It's a legacy, Marcus. And it's going to make you partner."

The word—*legacy*—landed with a satisfying weight. This was the culmination of everything he had worked for: the long nights in architecture school, the years of paying his dues, the strategic navigation of corporate politics in a predominantly white firm. Senior partner wasn't just a title; it was validation. It was proof that the boy from the small North Carolina town had not just made it, but had conquered the city.

Just as the meeting concluded with handshakes and satisfied smiles, his private line buzzed. His assistant's voice was apologetic. "Marcus, I'm sorry to interrupt. It's Keisha Daniels. She said it's urgent."

Marcus's professional composure faltered. Keisha wouldn't call his work line unless...

He took the call. The voice belonged to Keisha Daniels, though he almost didn't recognize it beneath the weight of exhaustion and grief. "I'm sorry to call you at work, but... your father asked me to. Ruth passed this morning."

The words hit him like cold water. The meticulously crafted model on his desk blurred as tears he hadn't expected gathered behind his eyes. Ruth Washington Johnson—the woman who had raised him to believe that education was liberation, that dignity was non-negotiable—was gone. The phone slipped in his suddenly nerveless fingers. The waterfront development, his legacy, suddenly felt small and meaningless.

He had been preparing himself for this call, had thought he was ready. The cancer had been aggressive and unforgiving. But hearing the news still felt like being unmoved from everything solid, cast adrift in a world that suddenly seemed less reliable without the woman who had been his moral compass for thirty-five years.

"When?" he asked, struggling to keep his voice professional.

"About an hour ago," Keisha replied, her own voice thick with tears. "Peaceful, at home... He kept asking about you, Marcus. Kept saying he hoped you'd come home for the service."

Home. The word landed strangely in Marcus's chest. Durham hadn't felt like home for a long time—it was the place he visited out of duty, the source of stories he told at dinner parties about growing up in the civil rights movement.

"Of course I'll come," he said, already mentally rearranging his schedule. "Tell them I'll need to reschedule," he told his assistant moments later, gesturing vaguely at the model. "Family emergency. I'll be out for the rest of the week."

The drive to Durham took five hours, winding through North Carolina countryside that looked exactly the same as it had when he was a child. He turned off the phone as he crossed into Durham County, needing silence to prepare himself for whatever emotions would surface when he walked into the house where Ruth had spent her final months.

The house looked smaller than he remembered, the one-story brick ranch his parents had bought in the 1980s. David met him at the front door, looking every one of his seventy-two years but still carrying himself with the dignity that had been Ruth's first attraction to him. The embrace they shared was longer than their usual greeting, both men understanding that something essential had changed.

The living room walls were covered with photographs spanning Ruth's sixty-seven years. He moved through the room accepting condolences from people who had known him as a child but now regarded him with a mixture of pride and puzzlement.

"Marcus, baby, I'm so sorry about your mama," Mother Caldwell said, approaching with the careful steps of someone whose ninety-eight years had earned her the right to speak truth without apology. "Your mama was proud of you," she continued, her ancient eyes studying his face. "But she worried about you too. Worried that success might make you forget where you came from, who raised you, what you were put on this earth to do."

The comment stung because it contained enough truth to pierce through the professional confidence Marcus had spent years cultivating. He had, if he was honest, allowed the story of his upbringing to become performance rather than foundation.

"I haven't forgotten," he said, though the words felt hollow.

"Good," Mother Caldwell replied, patting his arm. "She used to say that success without memory was just a fancy way of being lost."

The days that followed were a blur of shared memories and quiet grief. On the afternoon before the funeral, seeking a moment of solitude, Marcus walked to Mount Zion. The building sagged with a weariness that felt new to him. His professional eye, trained to notice every flaw, saw it all: water stains on the ceiling, cracks in the plaster, electrical fixtures decades out of date.

He ran his hand along the altar rail his great-grandfather had built. Kneeling down, he examined the foundation stones near the pulpit, the granite blocks that had survived two fires. As he traced the mortar line of a particularly large stone, his fingers brushed against something that wasn't rough stone. He looked closer. Carved into the mortar, almost invisible with age, were two tiny initials and a date: *S.W. 1951.*

Samuel Washington.

A jolt went through him. His great-grandfather had left his mark here, a hidden signature on the cornerstone of his faith. It was a tangible link, a whisper across seventy years. He was touching the same spot his great-grandfather had touched, a man who had built this place not for prestige, but for sanctuary. For the first time, Marcus didn't see a building in need of renovation; he saw a legacy in need of a steward.

That night, after the last of the visitors had departed, he found David on the porch swing.

"Your mama left some things for you," David said quietly. "Letters, mostly. But also some questions she hoped you'd think about."

"What kind of questions?" Marcus asked, a sense of dread mixing with curiosity.

"She wanted to know what you planned to do about Mount Zion," David said. He explained the crisis—the failing roof, the outdated electrical system, the insurance company threatening to cancel their policy. The estimated cost was a quarter of a million dollars, money the small, aging congregation simply did not have.

The weight of it settled on Marcus's shoulders like a heavy coat. This wasn't just a building; it was the physical embodiment of his family's legacy. The initials carved in the stone seemed to burn in his memory.

"What did Mama think we should do?" Marcus asked, needing her guidance one last time.

David managed a slight smile. "She thought you might have some ideas. She said you'd learned things in Atlanta about buildings and money and how to make impossible projects possible. But she also said you'd have to decide whether Mount Zion was worth saving, whether the community that raised you deserved the kind of help that only you were positioned to provide."

The challenge was vintage Ruth—practical and spiritual combined, a question about a building that was really a question about a life. Marcus looked out into the darkness, toward the faint silhouette of the church his great-grandfather had built. He thought of the waterfront development waiting for him in Atlanta, his monument to success. Then he thought of the initials, S.W., hidden in the foundation, a quiet testament to a different kind of legacy. The questions his mother had left for him were finally beginning to take shape, and he knew the answers would require more than architectural expertise. They would require a choice about what, and who, he was building for.

Wrestling with Angels

The rain that began falling on the morning of Ruth's burial continued for three days, turning the red clay soil of Durham into something that clung to shoes and stained clothes, as if the earth itself was reluctant to let go of the woman who had spent sixty-seven years nurturing everything she touched. Marcus stood at his childhood bedroom window, watching water pool in the low places of the yard where his father had taught him to throw a football, where his mother had planted flower beds that still bloomed according to her careful design despite her absence.

The funeral had been Tuesday. It was now Friday, and Marcus was supposed to be driving back to Atlanta, supposed to be returning to the waterfront development project that could secure his promotion to senior partner if he could just focus on billable hours instead of the growing recognition that his professional success felt increasingly hollow when measured against the standard of service that Ruth had modeled throughout her life.

Instead, he was sitting at the kitchen table where he had done homework under his mother's supervision, surrounded by boxes of her papers that David had asked him to help sort through—lesson plans spanning thirty years of teaching, letters from former students who had grown up to become nurses and mechanics and parents themselves, photographs from civil rights demonstrations where she had risked arrest for the principle that all people deserved equal treatment regardless of the color of their skin.

Each box contained evidence of a life organized around service to others, around the daily choice to invest in relationships that would never appear on any resume but that formed the actual foundation of a life worth living. Marcus found report cards she had saved from students who had struggled with reading, thank-you notes from parents whose children had flourished under her attention, newspaper clippings about former students who had gone on to achieve successes that their circumstances had not predicted.

"Your mama kept everything," David said, settling into his chair at the table with coffee that had become too strong from sitting on the burner all morning. Since Ruth's death, neither man had been able to maintain the domestic routines that she had organized with such efficiency—meals happened when hunger became impossible to ignore, laundry accumulated until clean clothes were no longer available, the small disciplines of daily life that had seemed automatic when Ruth was there to maintain them.

"She said you never knew when someone might need to remember that they had been important to somebody, that their work had mattered to people who cared enough to keep track of it."

Marcus opened another box and found himself looking at his own elementary school artwork, construction paper turkeys and handprint flowers that any reasonable person would have thrown away decades ago but that Ruth had preserved with the same care she gave to everything connected to the children she had loved. The sight hit him like a physical blow—not just the reminder of his mother's devotion, but the recognition of how far he had traveled from the boy who had created these simple projects with the confidence that someone would treasure them simply because he had made them.

When had he last created something with that kind of innocent faith in its reception? When had he last worked on a project because it brought joy rather than profit, because it served people he cared about rather than clients who could afford his fees but didn't particularly need his contribution to live dignified lives?

The questions burned in Marcus's chest as he continued sorting through Ruth's papers, encountering letter after letter from former students who credited her with changing the trajectory of their lives. One envelope contained a wedding invitation from a girl who had been in Ruth's first-grade class, along with a handwritten note explaining that she had become a teacher herself specifically because of Ruth's influence, that she was trying to provide the same kind of patient attention to struggling readers that had helped her discover her own love of learning.

Another box held correspondence from parents who had written to thank Ruth for seeing potential in children that others had dismissed as slow learners or behavior problems. The letters described transformations that had happened not through dramatic interventions but through the accumulation of small acts of attention—extra time spent on difficult concepts, phone calls to check on sick students, the kind of daily investment in human potential that required more faith than evidence, more persistence than immediate reward.

"I don't understand how she did it," Marcus said, looking up from a folder of student evaluations that Ruth had written with the careful attention to detail that characterized everything she touched. "How she managed to see the best in every single child, how she found energy to invest in so many people when the system was giving her so little support."

David smiled with the particular mixture of pride and loss that had characterized his expression since Ruth's death, the look of someone who had been privileged to witness greatness up close but would now have to carry the memory of it alone. "Your mama understood something about time that most people never figure out," he said, his words carrying the weight of forty-five years of marriage to a woman whose approach to daily life had consistently challenged conventional assumptions about productivity and efficiency.

"She knew that the most important work doesn't happen according to schedules or deadlines. She knew that loving people is something you do in the moments between other things, in the spaces that most folks think don't count for much but that actually hold everything together."

The observation highlighted something that Marcus had been struggling to articulate since returning to Durham—the recognition that his professional practice had gradually trained him to think about time as a commodity to be maximized, relationships as assets to be leveraged, success as something to be accumulated rather than something to be shared. The architecture firm operated according to principles that measured value in billable hours and profit margins, that treated client service as a means to an end rather than an end in itself.

But Ruth's papers told a different story about the relationship between work and meaning, about the possibility of organizing professional life around service rather than advancement, around contribution to others' flourishing rather than accumulation of personal resources. The letters and photographs and carefully preserved student projects suggested that the most satisfying work happened when people found ways to use their gifts in direct service of human needs, when expertise was offered as gift rather than commodity.

The afternoon brought a visit from Keisha, who arrived with takeout from the barbecue place that had been feeding Durham families for three generations and the expectation that men left to their own devices after losing the woman who had organized their domestic lives would need intervention to maintain basic nutrition. She took one look at the kitchen table covered with Ruth's papers and understood immediately what was happening—not just the practical work of sorting through accumulated possessions, but the emotional work of processing a legacy that felt both inspiring and overwhelming.

"Finding anything interesting?" she asked, settling into Ruth's chair with the easy familiarity of someone who had spent countless hours in this kitchen, who had been mentored and mothered by Ruth during the years when her own life felt too chaotic for clear direction.

"Finding out how much I don't know about the person who raised me," Marcus replied, gesturing toward the boxes that seemed to multiply rather than diminish despite hours of sorting. "I thought I understood what Mom's work was about, but these papers... they show somebody who was doing things I never even knew about, touching lives in ways that never made it into dinner table conversations."

Keisha nodded with the recognition of someone who had benefited from Ruth's behind-the-scenes generosity, who had been the recipient of the kind of attention that Ruth provided without fanfare or expectation of recognition. "Miss Ruth didn't do that work for praise," she said, opening containers of food with the efficiency of someone accustomed to caring for people who were too absorbed in grief to remember practical needs like eating regular meals.

"She did it because it needed doing and she had gifts that could do it. Same reason she taught Sunday school and organized the Christmas program and made sure elderly church members got to their medical appointments. She saw needs that weren't being met and figured out ways to meet them."

The simplicity of Keisha's explanation highlighted the complexity of Marcus's current situation—living in a city where individual success was celebrated more than collective well-being, working in a profession that served wealthy clients more than community needs, building a career that had gradually disconnected him from the values that had shaped his understanding of what made life worth living.

"Keisha," he said, surprising himself with the directness of his question, "do you think it's possible for someone like me to change? To find ways to use my skills for the kind of work Mom did, but in my own field?"

She studied his face with the attention of someone evaluating sincerity rather than just politeness, the same careful assessment that social workers learned to make when determining whether people were ready to do the difficult work of changing their lives in fundamental ways. "I think it's possible," she said finally, "but I also think it would require giving up some things that you've worked hard to achieve. The question is whether you're ready to make that trade."

The conversation was interrupted by Marcus's phone, which had been buzzing with increasing urgency throughout the afternoon. His assistant in Atlanta was calling to remind him about the Monday morning presentation to the zoning board, the proposal that would determine whether the waterfront development project moved forward and whether Marcus's bid for senior partnership remained viable.

"I need to take this," Marcus said, stepping onto the back porch where he could speak privately about professional obligations that felt increasingly remote from the questions that Ruth's death had forced him to confront.

"Marcus, thank God," his assistant's voice carried the particular strain of someone trying to manage multiple crises while her boss was absent from the office. "The zoning board moved up the meeting to tomorrow morning. The developers are flying in tonight, and they're expecting you to present the revised plans that incorporate the environmental impact modifications."

Marcus felt his stomach drop as he realized what this meant—not just the immediate crisis of missing a presentation that could determine his professional future, but the larger recognition that his life had been organized around obligations that allowed no accommodation for the kind of extended mourning that his heart seemed to require, no space for the process of reflection and reorientation that his mother's death had initiated.

"Can we reschedule?" he asked, though he already knew the answer. The development project was operating on a timeline determined by financial markets and municipal bureaucracy, forces that showed no mercy for personal loss or family obligations. "I'm still dealing with family matters here."

"The developers won't reschedule," she replied with the apologetic tone of someone delivering news that would complicate everyone's life. "They've already rearranged their own schedules to accommodate the zoning board's availability. If you can't present tomorrow, they'll find another firm to handle the project."

The ultimatum was delivered politely but clearly—return immediately and focus on work that generated revenue, or accept that fifteen years of career building could be derailed by divided attention during a moment when professional advancement required complete commitment to obligations that had nothing to do with the values Ruth had spent her life modeling.

Marcus ended the call and stood on the back porch, looking out over the neighborhood where he had learned his first lessons about justice and mercy, where his mother had taught him that individual success only mattered when it served something larger than individual ambition. The choice before him felt like a test of whether those lessons had taken root deeply enough to survive the practical pressures of adult life, whether the values he claimed to embrace were strong enough to guide decisions when choosing them carried real costs.

Through the kitchen window, he could see David and Keisha still sitting at the table, surrounded by the evidence of Ruth's commitment to work that paid poorly but served essential human needs. They were discussing something that made David smile—the first genuine smile Marcus had seen from his father since Ruth's death—and he realized that they were planning something, organizing some response to loss that involved building rather than just mourning, contribution rather than just grief.

Marcus returned to the kitchen to find them poring over architectural drawings that he recognized as his own sketches of Mount Zion Baptist Church, the documentation he had created while assessing the building's structural problems and restoration needs. But they had added notes and modifications, ideas for how the sanctuary could be renovated to serve broader community functions while maintaining its identity as a house of worship.

"We were thinking," Keisha said, looking up from the drawings with the particular excitement of someone who had discovered a solution to problems that had seemed intractable, "about what your mom would want us to do with Mount Zion. Not just fix the roof and update the electrical system, but transform it into something that could serve the whole community the way she served individual students."

David pointed to sketches that showed the fellowship hall expanded to accommodate community meetings, the kitchen upgraded to support meal programs for elderly residents and working families, meeting rooms that could house after-school programs and job training workshops and the kind of social services that communities needed but that government agencies were no longer funded to provide adequately.

"It would be expensive," David acknowledged, his practical nature warring with the vision that was taking shape on paper. "More than the congregation could afford, more than we could raise through traditional fundraising. But if we could find grants, foundation support, maybe some individual donors who believed in what we were trying to do..."

Marcus studied the drawings and felt something stirring in his chest that he hadn't experienced since architecture school, when he had still believed that buildings could change the world by creating spaces where human potential could flourish regardless of the economic or social obstacles that limited people's opportunities. The renovation plan was ambitious but achievable, the kind of adaptive reuse project that could attract foundation funding while serving genuine community needs.

More than that, it was exactly the kind of work that could use his professional expertise in service of the values Ruth had taught him, that could provide a model for how individual success could serve collective flourishing rather than just personal advancement. The technical challenges were significant but not insurmountable; the real question was whether he was ready to risk his career trajectory for work that offered less certain financial returns but potentially greater social impact.

"This is beautiful," Marcus said, his voice carrying the weight of recognition that he was looking at more than architectural drawings—he was looking at a potential future that could align his professional capabilities with his deepest values, that could honor Ruth's legacy through the practical work of building something that would serve the community she had loved throughout her life.

"But it would require someone with architectural expertise to manage the project, to navigate the regulatory environment, to ensure that the renovation meets current building codes while preserving the historic character that makes Mount Zion special."

The implication hung in the air between them like an invitation that was also a challenge—the possibility that Marcus could return to Durham not just for extended visits but for the sustained work of community development, that he could use his skills to help solve problems that affected the people who had invested everything in his success.

"Are you asking what I think you're asking?" Marcus said, looking between David and Keisha with the recognition that they were offering him an opportunity to participate in exactly the kind of work that Ruth would have celebrated, that would require him to choose service over advancement, community needs over client preferences.

"We're asking whether you think your mama's investment in your education was meant to serve only paying customers in Atlanta," Keisha replied with the gentle directness that had characterized her approach to difficult conversations since they were teenagers. "We're asking whether you think there might be another way to measure success, one that includes the kind of impact Miss Ruth spent her life making."

The phone in Marcus's pocket buzzed with another call from Atlanta—his assistant with more urgent requests for decisions about the waterfront development project, more pressure to return immediately and focus on obligations that would determine whether his bid for partnership remained viable. But for the first time in fifteen years, Marcus found himself questioning whether the partnership was worth pursuing if it required abandoning the possibility of work that aligned with his deepest values.

He looked at the drawings spread across the kitchen table, at the vision of Mount Zion transformed into a community center that could provide services and support and hope to families who had been abandoned by larger economic and political systems. The project would be challenging and uncertain, would require grant writing and fundraising and the kind of community organizing that Ruth had specialized in, that had sustained Mount Zion through decades of crises and celebrations.

But it would also be work that used his gifts in direct service of human needs, that addressed problems affecting people he cared about rather than clients who could afford his fees but didn't particularly need his contribution to live dignified lives. It would be work that honored Ruth's legacy not just through sentiment but through the practical application of everything she had taught him about the relationship between individual success and collective responsibility.

"I need to make some phone calls," Marcus said, his words carrying the weight of decisions that would reshape not just his immediate schedule but his fundamental understanding of what kind of person he wanted to be, what kind of work was worthy of the gifts Ruth had helped him develop.

The conversation with his assistant was difficult but clarifying. Yes, missing the zoning board presentation would probably cost him the waterfront development project. Yes, requesting extended leave to handle "family business" would likely eliminate his chances for partnership this year, possibly permanently. Yes, the firm would need to reassign his clients and redistribute his responsibilities if he couldn't commit to returning immediately and focusing exclusively on work that generated revenue.

The conversation with the senior partners was more complicated, touching on questions of loyalty and professional commitment, on the understanding that architectural practice was a business that required consistent attention to client needs and profit margins. They were willing to grant him additional bereavement leave, but not indefinitely, not for the kind of extended absence that community development work would require.

By evening, Marcus had reached the conclusion that Ruth's death had been preparing him for—that he would need to choose between two different definitions of success, two different approaches to using the gifts he had been given. He could return to Atlanta and continue building a career that served wealthy clients while providing financial security but limited social impact. Or he could risk everything he had achieved for the possibility of work that served community needs while offering less certain economic returns but potentially greater personal satisfaction.

The choice felt like stepping into the biblical story of Jacob wrestling with the angel—a struggle that would mark him permanently, that would determine not just his professional future but his fundamental identity as someone who had been blessed with opportunities that carried obligations to serve something larger than individual advancement.

That night, Marcus sat in Mount Zion's empty sanctuary, surrounded by the accumulated prayers and struggles and hopes of people who had built this place from nothing but faith and community determination. The building felt different in the darkness—more intimate and more vast simultaneously, like a space where human questions could be asked honestly and divine responses could be received without the distractions of daily life.

He thought about Ruth's funeral service, about the testimonies from people whose lives had been shaped by her particular combination of high expectations and unconditional love. He thought about the boxes of student papers and thank-you letters, about the evidence of a life organized around service that extended far beyond job descriptions or professional obligations.

Most of all, he thought about the architectural drawings spread across the kitchen table, about the vision of Mount Zion transformed into a community center that could provide hope and support to families who needed both desperately. The project represented everything Ruth had taught him about the relationship between individual gifts and collective needs, about the possibility of using professional expertise in direct service of human flourishing.

By the time Marcus left the sanctuary, he had reached a decision that felt both terrifying and inevitable. He would return to Atlanta long enough to arrange an extended leave of absence, to transfer his clients to other associates, to begin the process of reshaping his professional life around community service rather than corporate advancement.

The choice would cost him the partnership track, would probably require accepting a significant reduction in income, would definitely mean explaining to colleagues and clients why someone would abandon a successful career for work that offered less prestige and financial security.

But it would also mean using his gifts in service of the master who had actually entrusted them to him—not the corporate clients who paid his fees but the community that had shaped his character, that had invested everything in the faith that individual success could become collective blessing if the successful remembered who they were and where they came from and why their gifts had been given to them in the first place.

Walking home through streets that held the accumulated memories of his childhood and adolescence, Marcus felt something shift in his chest that he recognized as the same excitement he had felt in architecture school, when he had still believed that buildings could change the world by creating spaces where human potential could flourish regardless of the obstacles that limited people's opportunities.

The work ahead would be challenging and uncertain, would require skills he had never developed and faith he wasn't sure he possessed. But it would also be work that honored Ruth's memory through practical service rather than sentimental tribute, work that could transform her legacy from inspiration to action.

Tomorrow he would begin the process of reshaping his life around the values she had taught him, around the understanding that individual success only mattered when it served something larger than individual ambition. The wrestling match with his own priorities was ending; the real work of building something worthy of Ruth Washington's investment was about to begin.

The rain had stopped, and stars were visible through the clearing clouds—the same stars that had inspired his childhood dreams of becoming an architect, that were now illuminating his adult commitment to using architecture in service of the community that had made his dreams possible. The boy who had absorbed lessons about justice and mercy in Mount Zion's Sunday school was finally ready to become the man those lessons had been preparing him to be.

The Weight of Professional Sacrifice

The Atlanta skyline looked different through Marcus's office window on Monday morning—less like a symbol of opportunity and more like a monument to priorities he was questioning with increasing urgency. The waterfront development presentation had proceeded without him, and the partners' meeting to discuss his future with the firm was scheduled for ten o'clock, giving him exactly two hours to prepare explanations for choices that felt both necessary and professionally suicidal.

His desk was covered with the accumulated work of fifteen years—awards for design excellence, photographs from groundbreaking ceremonies, newspaper clippings about projects that had transformed Atlanta's downtown corridor into playground for people wealthy enough to afford luxury condominiums and boutique hotels. The evidence of his success felt simultaneously precious and hollow, like trophies from competitions he was no longer sure were worth winning.

The phone call from Durham had come at six in the morning, David's voice rough with exhaustion and something that might have been desperation. Mount Zion's insurance company had delivered an ultimatum—complete the necessary safety renovations within sixty days or lose coverage that the church could not afford to replace. Without insurance, the building could not legally host public gatherings, effectively ending Mount Zion's existence as a functioning congregation.

"They know we can't raise that kind of money in two months," David had said, his words carrying the weight of someone watching a family legacy disappear through bureaucratic indifference rather than malicious intent. "They know that small congregations like ours don't have access to emergency funding, don't have wealthy members who can write large checks when crises develop."

The timeline was impossible unless someone with architectural expertise could expedite the permitting process, coordinate contractors, navigate the regulatory environment that could delay renovation projects for months when every week mattered. It was exactly the kind of crisis that Marcus's professional training had prepared him to handle, but only if he could focus exclusively on Mount Zion's needs instead of dividing attention between community service and client obligations.

The dilemma felt like a test of whether the values Ruth had taught him were strong enough to guide decisions when choosing them carried real costs, when service required sacrifice rather than just good intentions. Marcus could continue building his successful career while occasionally contributing pro bono work to projects like Mount Zion's renovation. Or he could risk everything he had achieved for the possibility of work that aligned his professional expertise with his deepest commitments to community service.

The partners' meeting began with the kind of polite concern that barely concealed professional irritation at having to address personnel issues during time that could be spent on billable client work. Marcus had worked with these men for eight years, had learned to speak their language of profit margins and market positioning, had successfully absorbed their understanding that architectural practice was primarily about generating revenue rather than solving social problems.

"Marcus, we understand you've experienced a significant loss," the senior partner began, his words carrying the practiced sympathy of someone who had delivered similar speeches to other associates whose personal crises had interfered with professional obligations. "We want to support you during this difficult time, but we also need to understand your commitment to the projects that depend on your expertise."

The waterfront development contract had been reassigned to another associate, Marcus learned, along with two other major projects that required consistent attention from lead architects who could focus on client needs without distraction from family obligations. The message was clear without being explicitly stated—personal problems that interfered with professional performance would not be accommodated indefinitely, regardless of their legitimacy or severity.

"I appreciate the firm's patience," Marcus replied, choosing his words carefully to communicate respect while preparing ground for requests that would probably sound unreasonable to people who measured professional commitment in billable hours and client retention rates. "But I need to request extended leave to handle estate matters that require my personal attention."

The euphemism felt cowardly even as he spoke it—estate matters that were actually community development work, personal attention that was actually the application of professional expertise to problems affecting people who could not afford market-rate architectural services. But he needed time to make this transition carefully, to arrange his departure in ways that would not burn bridges he might someday need to cross again.

The negotiation that followed was cordial but decisive. The firm could grant him a three-month unpaid leave of absence, but not the indefinite arrangement that community development work would require. His clients would need permanent reassignment rather than temporary coverage, his office would need to be reassigned to associates whose commitment to Atlanta practice was unambiguous.

Most significantly, the partnership track that had motivated fifteen years of career building was no longer available to someone whose professional priorities included extended absences for community service work that generated no revenue for the firm. The door was not being closed permanently, the senior partner explained, but it was being closed for the foreseeable future.

Marcus accepted the terms with relief that surprised him—not because losing partnership opportunities felt good, but because the clarity of choice eliminated months of uncertainty about whether he could maintain career advancement while also serving community needs that required sustained attention rather than occasional volunteer work.

The afternoon was spent transferring files and briefing colleagues who would inherit his projects, explaining design decisions and client relationships to architects who understood technical requirements but not the community context that had begun shaping Marcus's approach to professional practice. The waterfront development project would proceed without consideration of its impact on working-class families who lived in neighborhoods targeted for gentrification, luxury hotels would be built without regard for their effect on affordable housing availability.

It was exactly the kind of work Marcus had been doing without question for fifteen years—serving clients who could afford premium services while ignoring the social consequences of development that prioritized profit over community stability. The work was legal and profitable and professionally respectable, but it no longer felt worthy of the gifts Ruth had helped him develop, no longer aligned with the values she had taught him about the relationship between individual success and collective responsibility.

By evening, Marcus had completed the practical work of arranging his departure from his Atlanta practice and begun the emotional work of processing what this choice meant for his identity as someone who had spent his adult life building a career that was now being voluntarily abandoned for uncertain alternatives.

The phone call to Jennifer, his ex-wife, was more difficult than the professional negotiations had been. She listened to his explanation of the choice to leave partnership track for community development work with the particular silence of someone trying to understand decisions that seemed to contradict everything she thought she knew about his priorities and ambitions.

"Marcus, I don't understand," she said finally, her voice carrying the confusion of someone who had been married to him for five years but had apparently never recognized the values that Ruth's death had forced him to acknowledge. "You've worked so hard to get where you are. Why would you throw that away for volunteer work that won't even pay your living expenses?"

The question highlighted the distance that had grown between them during their marriage—not just the geographical distance that had contributed to their divorce, but the philosophical distance between someone who measured success in individual achievement and someone who was learning to measure it in community contribution.

"Because the work I've been doing doesn't feel like it's worth the cost anymore," Marcus replied, struggling to articulate insights that were still forming in his own understanding. "Because my mother spent her life showing me what it looks like to use your gifts in service of people who need them, and I've spent fifteen years using my gifts in service of people who already have more than they need."

The conversation continued for another hour, touching on practical concerns about financial security and professional reputation, on the emotional work of rebuilding identity around service rather than advancement. Jennifer was not unsympathetic, but she was also not convinced that abandoning successful career for community development work was anything more than grief-induced temporary insanity that Marcus would regret once the emotional intensity of his mother's death subsided.

Her skepticism was not unreasonable—Marcus himself was not entirely certain that he was making wise decisions rather than just dramatic gestures that would prove impractical when community service work turned out to require skills he didn't possess, patience he hadn't developed, faith he wasn't sure he could maintain when the initial enthusiasm for radical career change gave way to daily frustration with slow progress and inadequate funding.

But he was certain that continuing to build a career that served primarily his own advancement while ignoring the community needs that Ruth had devoted her life to addressing would be a betrayal of everything she had taught him about the purpose of individual gifts, the relationship between success and service, the responsibility that came with being blessed with opportunities that others had been denied.

The packing of his Atlanta apartment took three days, not because he owned so many possessions but because each item required decisions about what kind of life he was preparing to live in Durham, what kind of person he was committing to become through choices that would reshape his daily routines around community service rather than professional advancement.

The furniture was too expensive and too formal for the house he would be sharing with David, at least temporarily, while they worked on Mount Zion's renovation and his own transition from architectural practice to community development work. The suits were wrong for the kind of work that involved construction sites and community meetings and fund-raising events where authenticity mattered more than professional polish.

But the books were right—volumes on architectural history and urban planning, on community development and historic preservation, on the kind of interdisciplinary approaches that would be required to transform Mount Zion from struggling congregation to community resource center. The professional library he had accumulated over fifteen years would serve different purposes in Durham, would be applied to problems affecting people who could not afford to hire experts but desperately needed expert attention.

The drawings were right too—sketches and renderings from projects that had taught him about adaptive reuse of historic buildings, about creative financing for community development initiatives, about the regulatory environment that governed renovation projects in small Southern towns. The technical knowledge would transfer, even if the context was dramatically different from luxury hotels and upscale condominiums.

Most importantly, the questions were right—the professional curiosity about how buildings could serve human flourishing, how architectural expertise could address social problems, how individual gifts could contribute to collective well-being rather than just personal advancement. The questions Ruth had taught him to ask about the relationship between success and service, about the purpose of individual achievement in communities where many people struggled to access basic necessities.

The drive from Atlanta to Durham took five hours, but it felt like traveling between different worlds rather than just different cities. The landscape was familiar—tobacco fields and pine forests, small towns that seemed frozen in time except for the chain restaurants and big box stores that had replaced local businesses that once provided employment and community gathering spaces.

But Marcus's perspective was different now, shaped by commitment to work that would require him to understand these communities from the inside rather than observing them from the highway during visits home for holidays and funerals. He would need to learn about local politics and funding sources, about the informal networks of mutual support that sustained people through economic hardship, about the particular challenges facing rural Southern communities that had been abandoned by manufacturing industries but not by the people who had built their lives around work that no longer existed.

The Mount Zion renovation project would be his introduction to community development work, his opportunity to discover whether architectural expertise could serve social justice goals when applied with patience and creativity rather than just technical competence. But it would also be his chance to honor Ruth's legacy through practical service rather than sentimental tribute, to use his gifts in direct response to needs that affected people who had invested everything in his success.

David was waiting on the front porch when Marcus pulled into the driveway, his father's face carrying the mixture of pride and concern that had characterized his expression since learning about his son's decision to abandon partnership track for community service work. The choice was risky and uncertain, would require faith in outcomes that could not be guaranteed, would definitely mean explaining to neighbors and church members why someone would leave successful career for work that offered less prestige and financial security.

But it would also mean daily collaboration with his father on work that honored Ruth's memory, daily application of professional skills to problems that had kept her awake at night worrying about the church community she had served for forty years. The renovation project would transform Mount Zion from struggling congregation to community resource center, would create space for the kind of programs and services that Ruth had organized informally but that needed institutional support to reach their full potential.

"Welcome home, son," David said, embracing Marcus with the warmth that came from understanding that this homecoming was different from previous visits—not temporary retreat from professional obligations but permanent commitment to work that aligned individual gifts with community needs, that honored Ruth Washington's investment in her son's education by applying that education to problems affecting people who had supported his success from the beginning.

The evening was spent reviewing architectural drawings and renovation plans, discussing funding strategies and contractor relationships, preparing for work that would require more than technical expertise—would require the kind of community organizing skills that Ruth had possessed, the ability to mobilize resources and coordinate volunteers and maintain hope through setbacks that would inevitably complicate every aspect of the project.

But Marcus felt ready for challenges that would test more than his professional competence, that would require the kind of faith Ruth had modeled throughout her life—faith that individual gifts were meant to serve collective needs, that community problems could be solved through sustained effort and creative collaboration, that some work was worth doing regardless of its impact on personal advancement or financial security.

The wrestling match with his own priorities was ending, and the real work of building something worthy of Ruth Washington's legacy was about to begin. Outside, the night sky stretched over Durham with the same stars that had inspired his childhood dreams of becoming an architect, that were now illuminating his adult commitment to using architecture in service of the community that had made his dreams possible.

Tomorrow would bring the practical challenges of community development work—grant applications and contractor negotiations, community meetings and fundraising events, the daily discipline of choosing service over comfort. But tonight there was only the satisfaction of finally aligning his professional capabilities with his deepest values, of discovering that coming home could be about more than visiting the past—it could be about building a future that honored everything the past had taught him about who he was meant to become.

New Wine, Old Wineskins

The morning of Mount Zion's emergency congregation meeting dawned clear and cold, the kind of February day that made the sanctuary's broken heating system feel less like inconvenience than genuine hardship. Marcus arrived early to set up folding chairs borrowed from the funeral home, his breath visible in the frigid air as he arranged seating for what he hoped would be enough people to constitute a quorum for the decisions that needed to be made.

Six weeks had passed since his return from Atlanta, six weeks of grant applications and contractor estimates, of community meetings and fundraising events that had raised more questions than money. The insurance company's sixty-day ultimatum had been extended through negotiations that cost more than the congregation could afford, but the underlying crisis remained: Mount Zion needed a quarter million dollars in renovations or it would close permanently, its seventy-year history reduced to memories and whatever artifacts could be preserved in members' homes.

The architectural plans spread across the altar rail told a different story—Marcus's vision of the church transformed into a community center that could serve the entire neighborhood rather than just the dwindling congregation. The fellowship hall expanded to accommodate community meetings, the kitchen upgraded to support meal programs for elderly residents and working families, meeting rooms that could house after-school programs and job training workshops and the kind of social services that communities needed but that government agencies were no longer funded to provide adequately.

It was an ambitious plan that could attract foundation funding and individual donations from people who believed in community development work. But it was also expensive and uncertain, requiring the kind of leap of faith that small congregations had learned to avoid after decades of watching good intentions collide with financial reality.

David arrived carrying coffee and the weight of his own complicated emotions about what this meeting might decide, whether the church his father-in-law had built from nothing but faith and community determination would survive to serve another generation or whether economic pressures would finally accomplish what two fires had failed to achieve.

"How many people are you expecting?" David asked, surveying the sixty chairs that Marcus had arranged in concentric semicircles facing the altar where Pastor Williams would present the renovation proposal alongside the grim alternative of permanent closure.

"Enough to make the right decision," Marcus replied, though he wasn't sure what the right decision looked like when all available options carried risks that could destroy what three generations of his family had worked to build and preserve.

The congregation members began arriving at ten o'clock sharp, faces that carried the accumulated wisdom of people who had survived repeated crises through careful evaluation of practical realities rather than romantic attachment to beautiful ideas. Mother Caldwell took her customary place in the front row, her ninety-eight years having earned her the right to speak first and be heard completely whenever church business required community discernment.

Angela Martinez settled into a seat near the middle, her presence representing the newer members who had found spiritual home at Mount Zion but whose financial resources were limited by student loans and entry-level salaries and the economic realities facing young adults who had grown up in communities where traditional employment opportunities had largely disappeared.

The Johnson family filled an entire pew—three generations who had been baptized in Mount Zion's sanctuary, whose children had learned to read in the church's Sunday school program, whose family celebrations and funeral services had been held in fellowship halls that were now threatened by structural problems that had been accumulating for decades.

Marcus counted forty-three people by the time Pastor Williams called the meeting to order with a prayer that asked for wisdom rather than miracles, for discernment that could distinguish between faithful risk-taking and foolish presumption. The congregation was older than it had been during Marcus's childhood, grayer and smaller, marked by the absence of young families who had left Durham for cities that offered better educational and economic opportunities for their children.

But it was also the core group that had sustained Mount Zion through previous crises, the people who had organized fish fries and bake sales to keep the lights on when utility bills exceeded weekly offerings, who had contributed volunteer labor when the church couldn't afford professional contractors, who had maintained faith that solutions would emerge if people simply refused to give up.

"Brothers and sisters," Pastor Williams began, his voice carrying the authority of someone who had learned to deliver difficult news with honesty that preserved hope rather than destroying it, "we gather this morning to make decisions about Mount Zion's future that will affect not just our congregation but the entire community that has been served by this ministry for more than seventy years."

The insurance ultimatum was explained in detail—the safety violations that had accumulated over decades of deferred maintenance, the liability issues that made continued public gatherings legally problematic, the timeline that made traditional fundraising approaches inadequate for addressing problems that required immediate attention rather than gradual solutions.

But the alternative was also presented with equal clarity—Marcus's vision of Mount Zion transformed into a community resource center that could attract grant funding while serving the neighborhood's practical needs, that could ensure the church's survival by expanding its mission beyond weekly worship services to encompass the kind of daily community support that Ruth Washington had provided informally but that needed institutional backing to reach its full potential.

"The question before us," Pastor Williams continued, "is whether we believe God is calling us to take risks for the sake of ministry that could serve more people than we've ever been able to serve, or whether faithful stewardship requires us to accept closure rather than pursuing dreams that might be too expensive for our resources."

The discussion that followed was passionate but respectful, touching on questions of theology and practical economics, on the relationship between individual faith and collective responsibility, on what it meant to honor previous generations' sacrifices while adapting to circumstances they could never have anticipated.

Mother Caldwell spoke first, her voice carrying the authority of someone who had witnessed Mount Zion's construction and reconstruction, who had participated in every major decision the congregation had made since the 1950s. "This church has been destroyed twice by people who thought they could stop our faith by burning our building," she said, her words settling over the gathered congregation like benediction and challenge combined. "Both times we rebuilt because we understood that our sanctuary was not made of wood and brick but of the people who gathered here to worship God and serve each other. This insurance crisis is just another kind of fire, and we need to decide whether we're going to let it destroy what previous generations died to preserve."

The theological argument was compelling, but the financial realities were daunting. Mrs. Patterson's daughter raised her hand to ask about the specific fundraising targets that would be required to implement Marcus's renovation plan, about the timeline for securing grants and donations that could supplement whatever the congregation could contribute through traditional methods.

Marcus stood to present the detailed financial analysis he had prepared, the spreadsheets and projections that translated architectural vision into practical requirements. The total project cost was $280,000—more money than most of the congregation members would see in their lifetimes, but not impossible to raise through combination of foundation grants, individual donations, and low-interest loans from denominational sources that supported community development initiatives.

"The key is demonstrating community impact," Marcus explained, clicking through slides that showed similar projects in other Southern towns, churches that had successfully transformed themselves into community resource centers while maintaining their identity as houses of worship. "Foundations want to fund work that serves more than just congregation members, that addresses genuine social needs in sustainable ways."

The community impact would be substantial—after-school programs for children whose parents worked multiple jobs, job training workshops for adults displaced by economic changes, community meals for elderly residents and working families, meeting space for neighborhood organizations and support groups. Mount Zion could become what Ruth Washington had been individually—a source of practical help and spiritual encouragement for anyone who needed both.

But the risks were equally substantial. If the fundraising campaign failed to reach its targets, if grants didn't materialize or donors didn't respond as hoped, the congregation could lose not just the building but the modest savings and investments that would be required as matching funds for foundation support.

James Wilson raised his hand to voice concerns that several others shared—whether a congregation of forty-three mostly elderly members could manage the kind of expanded programming that the community center model would require, whether they had the energy and expertise to serve the broader neighborhood when they were already struggling to maintain basic church operations.

"We barely have enough volunteers to keep the Sunday school program running," he pointed out with the practical honesty that had characterized his approach to church leadership for two decades. "How are we going to staff after-school programs and community meals and all the other services that Marcus is proposing?"

It was a fair question that touched on the fundamental challenge facing small congregations throughout the South—how to expand ministry when existing resources were already stretched to their limits, how to serve growing community needs with declining membership and aging leadership.

Marcus had anticipated the concern and prepared a response that drew on his research into other successful community center projects. "The expanded programming wouldn't be staffed entirely by church members," he explained. "Part of the grant funding would support hiring professional staff—social workers, program coordinators, people with expertise in community development work."

The church members would provide oversight and spiritual foundation, but the daily operations would be managed by people whose job it was to coordinate volunteers from throughout the community, to develop partnerships with other organizations, to ensure that programs served their intended purposes effectively and sustainably.

Angela Martinez raised her hand to offer a perspective that bridged the generational gap between long-term members and newer participants in Mount Zion's ministry. "I think we need to ask ourselves what Miss Ruth would want us to do," she said, her words carrying the weight of personal experience with Ruth's approach to community service.

"Miss Ruth never waited for perfect circumstances before she started helping people. She saw needs and figured out ways to meet them, even when she didn't have adequate resources or institutional support. This renovation project feels like the same kind of faithful risk-taking that she modeled throughout her life."

The comment shifted the discussion from practical concerns to spiritual discernment, from questions about feasibility to questions about calling, from risk assessment to trust in divine provision that had sustained Mount Zion through previous crises that had seemed equally impossible to overcome.

Pastor Williams opened the floor for testimonies from congregation members who wanted to share their own sense of what God was asking them to do in response to the current crisis, what faithfulness looked like when choosing between certain closure and uncertain expansion.

Mrs. Henderson spoke about her granddaughter, who lived in the housing project three blocks from Mount Zion and whose children needed after-school supervision while she worked two jobs to support the family. The community center model would provide exactly the kind of programming that could help children succeed academically while giving working parents peace of mind about their safety and care.

Deacon Thompson talked about his own experience with unemployment after the textile mill closure, about the months of searching for work that paid living wages and provided health insurance for families with mortgages and car payments and all the obligations that came with middle-class life that had been built on the assumption of steady employment.

The job training workshops that Marcus's plan proposed could provide practical skills for people who needed to reinvent their careers in their fifties and sixties, who were willing to learn new trades but needed institutional support to access training programs and certification requirements.

The testimonies continued for nearly an hour, each story illustrating the community needs that Mount Zion could address through expanded programming, the practical ways that faith could be expressed through social services that helped people navigate economic hardship and family crises and the various forms of struggle that seemed to accumulate when larger systems failed to provide adequate support.

But the testimonies also revealed the congregation's own needs—for purpose and relevance in a community where traditional church attendance was declining, for ways to honor Ruth Washington's legacy through service rather than just memory, for hope that their investments in faith and community would continue paying dividends for future generations.

Mother Caldwell asked for the floor again as the testimony period drew to a close, her request granted immediately by people who understood that her words would carry special weight in whatever decision-making process followed. She stood slowly, her ancient frame supported by a walker but her voice clear and strong as it had been for ninety-eight years of speaking truth in love.

"I want to tell you young people something about building churches," she said, her gaze moving across faces that included congregation members in their sixties who were still young compared to her accumulated experience. "Every time we've built or rebuilt Mount Zion, people said we were being foolish, taking risks we couldn't afford, dreaming dreams that were too big for our resources."

She paused, letting the historical perspective settle into minds that had heard similar concerns about the current renovation proposal, that were struggling with the same tension between prudent stewardship and faithful risk-taking that had faced previous generations of church leadership.

"But we built anyway, because we understood that faith without works is dead, that believing in God's provision requires us to act like we actually believe rather than just hoping things will work out without our participation. This community center plan is the same kind of faithful work—risky but necessary, expensive but valuable, uncertain but aligned with everything we claim to believe about God's call to serve others."

The silence that followed Mother Caldwell's comments was thick with recognition that the decision before them was about more than building renovation or financial planning—it was about identity, about what kind of congregation they wanted to be, about whether their faith was strong enough to support the kind of expansion that could serve community needs while requiring unprecedented levels of trust in outcomes that could not be guaranteed.

Pastor Williams called for a brief recess before the formal vote, giving congregation members time to pray privately and consider the choice between accepting closure or pursuing renovation that could ensure Mount Zion's survival while transforming its ministry in fundamental ways.

Marcus stepped outside for fresh air and found himself joined by several congregation members who wanted to ask specific questions about the renovation timeline, about his own commitment to seeing the project through completion, about what would happen if fundraising fell short of projected targets.

The questions were practical and necessary, reflecting the kind of careful evaluation that responsible church leadership required when making decisions that would affect not just current members but future generations of people who might benefit from expanded community services.

But they were also questions that touched on Marcus's own uncertainties about whether he possessed the skills and patience required for community development work, whether his architectural expertise would prove adequate for the complex challenge of transforming struggling congregation into thriving community resource center.

"I can't guarantee success," Marcus said honestly, addressing concerns that several people had raised about his experience with grant writing and nonprofit management, about whether someone trained in corporate architectural practice could adapt to the very different requirements of community organizing and social service delivery.

"But I can guarantee commitment. This project isn't something I'm doing in my spare time between more important work—it's become the most important work, the way I want to honor my mother's legacy and use the gifts that this community helped me develop."

The conversation was interrupted by Keisha Daniels, who arrived carrying folders full of documentation that she had been preparing for weeks—letters of support from other community organizations, preliminary commitments from potential funding sources, examples of successful church-to-community-center transitions that demonstrated the viability of Marcus's proposal.

"Sorry I'm late," she said, though her arrival felt more like divine timing than tardiness. "I wanted to make sure we had all the information we needed before making this decision."

Keisha's presence shifted the dynamic of the gathering, her reputation as effective community organizer lending credibility to the renovation proposal that pure architectural expertise might not have provided. She had been working behind the scenes to build support for the project, reaching out to foundations and individual donors, developing partnerships with other organizations that could share programming responsibilities and operational costs.

"The Kellogg Foundation has indicated interest in funding the after-school programming," she reported, opening folders that contained letters and preliminary agreements that transformed Marcus's vision from hopeful proposal to practical possibility. "The Community Development Corporation is willing to provide matching funds for the job training workshops, and the Department of Social Services wants to establish a satellite office in the renovated fellowship hall."

The news energized the congregation in ways that architectural drawings and financial projections had not, providing evidence that external organizations shared their assessment of the project's value, that the expanded programming would serve genuine community needs rather than just congregation dreams.

But it also increased the pressure to make decisions quickly, while funding opportunities were available and organizational partnerships could be formalized, before external support moved on to other projects that were ready to proceed immediately rather than waiting for internal church politics to reach consensus.

When the congregation reconvened for the formal vote, the atmosphere had changed from cautious evaluation to cautious optimism, from fear of risk to recognition that failing to act carried its own risks, that choosing safety might mean choosing slow death rather than uncertain life.

Pastor Williams explained the voting procedure—a simple yes or no decision about whether to proceed with Marcus's renovation proposal, understanding that yes meant committing to aggressive fundraising campaign and expanded ministry that would require more energy and faith than the congregation had ever invested in any single project.

The vote was conducted by secret ballot, giving members freedom to follow their conscience without pressure from neighbors or family members, without concern about disappointing people whose opinions they valued but whose financial commitment they could not guarantee.

Marcus felt his heart hammering as Pastor Williams counted ballots with the careful attention that democratic decisions required, the recognition that this vote would determine not just Mount Zion's future but his own professional trajectory, his ability to honor Ruth's legacy through practical service rather than sentimental tribute.

"The vote is thirty-seven in favor, six opposed," Pastor Williams announced, his voice carrying relief and excitement in equal measure. "Mount Zion Baptist Church will proceed with the community center renovation project."

The congregation erupted in applause that felt more like celebration than mere approval, recognition that they had chosen faith over fear, expansion over contraction, risk over the false safety of managed decline. But the applause also carried acknowledgment that the real work was just beginning, that voting to proceed was easier than raising funds and coordinating contractors and managing the hundreds of details that would determine whether their faith-based decision produced practical results.

Marcus felt tears starting in his eyes as he accepted congratulations from congregation members who had just voted to trust him with the most important project in Mount Zion's history, who had chosen to believe that his architectural expertise could serve their community development goals, that individual success could become collective blessing when applied with sufficient commitment and creativity.

But the tears were not just relief or gratitude—they were also recognition that he had finally found work that aligned his professional capabilities with his deepest values, that honored Ruth Washington's investment in his education by applying that education to problems affecting people who had supported his success from the beginning.

The afternoon was spent in practical planning—forming committees to oversee different aspects of the renovation project, establishing timelines for grant applications and contractor negotiations, dividing responsibilities among congregation members who possessed different skills and resources but shared common commitment to seeing the project through to completion.

Marcus would serve as project coordinator, managing architectural and construction issues while working with Keisha on fundraising and community outreach, with Pastor Williams on programming development and volunteer coordination. It was exactly the kind of collaborative leadership that Ruth had modeled throughout her life, the understanding that complex challenges required diverse expertise rather than individual heroics.

But it was also the kind of leadership that Marcus had never practiced, the patient work of building consensus and maintaining morale through setbacks that would inevitably complicate every aspect of the project. His corporate architectural practice had taught him to make decisions quickly and implement them efficiently, but community development work required different skills—the ability to listen more than speak, to coordinate rather than control, to trust collective wisdom rather than individual expertise.

As the meeting concluded and congregation members began heading home to families and responsibilities, Marcus remained in the sanctuary that would soon be transformed according to plans he had drawn but that belonged to the entire community, that represented shared vision rather than individual achievement.

The late afternoon light slanted through stained glass windows that depicted biblical scenes in colors that would be preserved and protected during renovation, historical artifacts that connected Mount Zion's future to its past, that ensured continuity of identity even as programming expanded to serve community needs in new ways.

David joined him in the quiet sanctuary, settling into a pew that had held him through decades of worship services and committee meetings, celebrations and crises that had tested and strengthened his faith in equal measure. "Your mama would be proud," he said simply, his words carrying the weight of someone who had known Ruth well enough to speak with confidence about her probable response to the day's decisions.

Marcus nodded, understanding that Ruth's pride would be less about architectural achievement than about community service, less about professional success than about the choice to use individual gifts in direct response to collective needs. The renovation project honored her legacy not through monument building but through practical application of lessons she had taught about the relationship between faith and works, between believing and doing.

The work ahead would be challenging and uncertain, would require skills Marcus was still developing and patience he wasn't sure he possessed. But it would also be work that demonstrated daily commitment to values Ruth had modeled throughout her life—that individual achievement only mattered when it served something larger than individual advancement, that professional expertise was most valuable when applied to problems affecting people who needed help but couldn't afford to purchase it.

Outside, the February evening settled over Durham with the promise of spring that was still weeks away but already visible in the lengthening daylight, the subtle changes that marked winter's gradual retreat. The community that had invested everything in Marcus's education was about to benefit from that investment in ways that measured success not in individual advancement but in collective flourishing, not in personal achievement but in shared hope made practical through patient work and stubborn faith.

Tomorrow would bring the real challenges of community development work—grant applications that required expertise Marcus was still acquiring, contractor negotiations that demanded skills Ruth had never needed to teach him, fundraising events that would test his ability to communicate vision in ways that moved hearts as well as minds.

But tonight there was only the satisfaction of finally aligning his professional capabilities with his deepest commitments, of discovering that coming home could be about building the future rather than just visiting the past, of honoring his mother's memory through service that would outlast any monument that stone and mortar could provide.

The boy who had absorbed lessons about justice and mercy in Mount Zion's Sunday school was finally ready to become the man those lessons had been preparing him to be—not perfect or completely prepared, but committed to work that mattered more than success, to service that honored the best of what he had inherited while building something worthy of what he hoped to pass forward to the next generation of children who would need to know that their dreams were worth pursuing regardless of the obstacles they might encounter.

The wrestling match with his own priorities was ending, and the real work of building something beautiful from community commitment and individual gifts was about to begin.

The grant writing consumed Marcus's life for the next three weeks, transforming his childhood bedroom into a cramped office where foundation application deadlines competed for attention with contractor estimates and architectural drawings that needed constant revision to meet funders' requirements. Each application demanded a slightly different approach—the Kellogg Foundation wanted detailed youth development programming, while the Ford Foundation emphasized community capacity building, and the Methodist denomination required extensive theological justification for transforming worship space into multiuse facility.

Marcus had never realized how much community development work resembled translation—taking the same basic vision and expressing it in languages that different audiences could understand and support. The architectural drawings that spoke clearly to contractors needed accompanying narratives that explained social impact to program officers who had never seen rural Southern poverty firsthand, who needed statistics and case studies to understand why after-school programming mattered to children whose parents worked multiple jobs without benefits or job security.

The kitchen table became mission control for the fundraising campaign, covered with spreadsheets tracking foundation deadlines and individual donor prospects, with correspondence from organizations that might provide matching funds or in-kind services, with the accumulated paperwork of turning vision into reality through the patient work of documentation and persuasion.

David worked alongside him, applying decades of experience with church fundraising to the more complex requirements of grant writing and major donor cultivation. His father possessed skills that Marcus was still learning—how to tell stories that moved hearts as well as minds, how to maintain hope through rejection letters that offered encouragement but no funding, how to celebrate small victories while keeping eyes focused on larger goals that required sustained effort rather than dramatic breakthroughs.

"Foundation work is like farming," David observed during one particularly frustrating afternoon when three applications had been rejected in a single day, each with polite explanations about limited funding and difficult choices among worthy projects. "You plant seeds in a lot of different fields, tend them as best you can, and trust that enough will grow to feed the people who are counting on the harvest."

The metaphor helped Marcus maintain perspective when grant writing felt more like gambling than strategic planning, when months of work could be dismissed with form letters that praised the project's merit while explaining that funding priorities had shifted or budgets had been reduced or other applications had better aligned with current strategic initiatives.

But the rejections also taught valuable lessons about how to strengthen future applications, how to better articulate community impact and organizational capacity, how to demonstrate that Mount Zion possessed the leadership and partnerships necessary to manage expanded programming effectively. Each rejection letter contained feedback that improved subsequent proposals, that helped Marcus learn to think like a foundation program officer evaluating dozens of requests for limited resources.

The breakthrough came from an unexpected source—a conversation with Jennifer during one of their increasingly rare phone calls, when she mentioned her employer's corporate foundation was looking for community development projects that could showcase their commitment to social responsibility while serving markets where they hoped to expand business operations.

"I know you think corporate funding comes with too many strings attached," she said, referencing arguments they had during their marriage about the relationship between business interests and genuine community service. "But sometimes the strings are reasonable, and the funding can make projects possible that wouldn't happen otherwise."

Marcus swallowed his pride and requested application materials from the corporation where Jennifer worked as marketing director, discovering that their community development priorities aligned surprisingly well with Mount Zion's renovation plans. They wanted projects that served working families, that provided job training and after-school programming, that demonstrated sustainable impact through measurable outcomes rather than just good intentions.

More importantly, they were willing to provide large grants to projects that could serve as models for similar initiatives in other markets, that could generate positive publicity while addressing genuine social needs. Mount Zion's history and Marcus's architectural expertise created exactly the kind of story that corporate communications departments could use to demonstrate authentic commitment to community investment.

The application process was rigorous but straightforward—less focused on theological justifications than secular foundations required, more interested in practical outcomes than denominational grants demanded. Marcus found himself translating Mount Zion's mission into business language that emphasized efficiency and measurable results, return on investment and strategic partnerships that could leverage corporate funding to attract additional resources.

The site visit was scheduled for a Thursday in March, when foundation representatives would tour the existing facility and meet with congregation members who would be affected by the renovation project. Marcus spent days preparing for questions about project management and financial oversight, about community support and organizational capacity, about his own qualifications for coordinating complex construction while managing expanded programming.

But the foundation representatives were more interested in stories than statistics, more concerned with authenticity than polish. They wanted to understand why this project mattered to people whose lives would be changed by after-school programming and job training workshops, community meals and support groups that addressed practical needs while building social connections that isolated people desperately needed.

Mother Caldwell's testimony was particularly powerful—not because she spoke eloquently about community development theory, but because she described with simple clarity how Mount Zion had sustained her through decades of personal and collective challenges, how the church had provided not just spiritual guidance but practical support during periods of unemployment and illness and family crisis.

"This renovation isn't about making our building fancier," she explained to foundation representatives who had seen hundreds of similar projects but rarely heard them described with such direct honesty. "It's about making sure the next generation of children has the same kind of sanctuary that kept us alive when staying alive required more faith than most people thought reasonable."

Angela Martinez spoke about her own transformation from grief-stricken daughter to community choir director, about discovering that broken people could still make beautiful music if they had safe spaces to practice healing together. The after-school programming would provide similar opportunities for children whose families were struggling with economic displacement, who needed adults to believe in their potential even when circumstances seemed to argue against hope.

James Wilson described his vision for job training workshops that could prepare unemployed adults for careers in building trades and healthcare support, fields that offered decent wages and growth opportunities for people willing to learn new skills but who needed institutional support to access certification programs and apprenticeship opportunities.

The testimonies painted a picture of community-centered development that addressed genuine needs through sustainable programming, that built on existing strengths rather than imposing external solutions, that honored local leadership while leveraging outside resources to expand impact beyond what any single congregation could achieve independently.

By the time the foundation representatives departed, Marcus felt cautiously optimistic about their response to the project proposal. The questions had been probing but supportive, focused on implementation details rather than fundamental project viability. The site visit had demonstrated community commitment and organizational capacity, had shown that Mount Zion possessed the leadership and partnerships necessary to manage expanded programming effectively.

The phone call came two weeks later, on a Tuesday morning when Marcus was reviewing contractor bids for the first phase of renovation work. The foundation program officer's voice carried the particular tone of someone delivering news that would change everything—Mount Zion had been awarded a $150,000 grant, enough to fund the major structural improvements while leaving room for additional funding from other sources.

More importantly, the foundation was willing to serve as lead funder, providing the kind of institutional credibility that could attract matching grants from other organizations that preferred to support projects with demonstrated viability rather than untested ventures. The corporate grant would catalyze additional funding rather than simply providing partial support for work that might never achieve full financing.

Marcus hung up the phone and felt something that was part relief, part terror—relief that months of grant writing had produced results, terror that success meant the real work was just beginning, that he now had to deliver on promises made during the application process, had to prove that his architectural expertise could serve community development goals as effectively as he had claimed.

The news spread through Mount Zion's congregation within hours, carried by phone calls and impromptu visits that transformed individual celebration into collective joy. The grant award meant more than financial support—it meant external validation of the project's merit, professional recognition that the renovation plans addressed genuine community needs through sustainable programming.

But it also meant increased pressure to execute the project flawlessly, to manage construction and programming development simultaneously, to coordinate volunteers and contractors and funding sources in ways that produced results worthy of the investment that multiple organizations were making in Mount Zion's vision.

The celebration that Sunday felt different from typical church services—less about worship and more about commissioning, less about receiving blessing and more about accepting responsibility for work that would affect not just congregation members but the entire community that had been promised programming and services that didn't yet exist.

Pastor Williams preached from the parable of the talents, about servants who had been entrusted with their master's resources and the different ways they chose to invest what they had been given. But this time the sermon felt less like moral instruction and more like practical guidance for people who were about to discover whether their faith was strong enough to support the kind of expansion that required unprecedented levels of commitment and creativity.

"We have been given resources that we didn't earn and don't deserve," Pastor Williams said, his words carrying across the sanctuary that would soon be transformed according to plans that existed only on paper and in the collective imagination of people who had voted to trust Marcus with the most important project in Mount Zion's history.

"The question is whether we will use these resources to serve ourselves or to serve others, whether we will bury our talents to keep them safe or invest them in work that multiplies blessing through the patient discipline of daily service to needs that we can see but cannot solve through individual effort alone."

Marcus listened to the sermon and felt the weight of inherited responsibility settling on his shoulders—not just architectural and financial responsibility, but spiritual responsibility for ensuring that the renovation project served the community development goals that had justified foundation support, that honored Ruth Washington's legacy through practical service rather than monument building.

The work ahead would require more than technical expertise—it would require the kind of community organizing skills that Ruth had possessed, the ability to mobilize resources and coordinate volunteers and maintain hope through setbacks that would inevitably complicate every aspect of the project.

But it would also require faith that individual gifts were meant to serve collective needs, that community problems could be solved through sustained effort and creative collaboration, that some work was worth doing regardless of its impact on personal advancement or professional recognition.

As the service concluded and congregation members began discussing practical next steps for launching the renovation project, Marcus felt something that was part excitement, part trepidation—the recognition that success would be measured not in architectural achievement but in community impact, not in professional recognition but in the daily evidence that expanded programming was actually serving families who needed support that had not been available before Mount Zion's transformation.

The boy who had absorbed lessons about justice and mercy in this same sanctuary was finally ready to become the man those lessons had prepared him to be—not through individual heroics but through collaborative leadership, not through dramatic gestures but through the patient work of turning vision into reality one day at a time, one relationship at a time, one small victory at a time.

The wrestling match with angels was ending, and the real work of building beloved community was about to begin.

When the Silence Speaks

The morning light filtered through the new stained glass windows of Mount Zion Baptist Church with a clarity that seemed impossible just eighteen months earlier, when the building had stood on the verge of condemnation and the congregation had faced the choice between faithful risk and managed decline. Marcus stood in the transformed sanctuary, watching dust motes dance in colored beams that fell across pews filled with more people than had gathered in this space for twenty years—not just congregation members, but neighbors and community partners, children and grandparents, the living testimony to what could happen when individual gifts were offered in service of collective dreams.

The dedication service was scheduled to begin in an hour, but Marcus had arrived early to walk through spaces that existed now in three dimensions rather than just architectural drawings, to see with his own eyes the evidence that vision could become reality when enough people decided that some things were worth building regardless of the obstacles that seemed to make building impossible.

The sanctuary itself remained recognizably Mount Zion—the altar rail where his great-grandfather had knelt in prayer, the baptismal font where three generations of his family had made public declarations of faith, the wooden cross that had survived two fires and countless smaller crises through the stubborn determination of people who refused to let hatred or economic hardship have the final word. But everything else spoke of transformation that honored the past while serving the future, that preserved sacred memory while creating space for sacred work that had never been possible within these walls.

The fellowship hall had been expanded to accommodate community meetings and social services, equipped with computers and tables that could serve everything from job training workshops to support groups for families dealing with addiction. The kitchen met commercial standards now, capable of preparing meals for the elderly nutrition program that served sixty people daily, the after-school snacks that sustained children whose parents worked multiple jobs, the community dinners that brought neighbors together around tables where differences in income and education mattered less than shared commitment to each other's well-being.

Most remarkably, the building buzzed with activity that had nothing to do with Sunday worship—children's laughter from the after-school program that occupied the renovated Sunday school rooms, adult voices from the job training workshop that met in the basement, the quiet conversations of people receiving assistance from the social services coordinator who maintained office hours in what had once been a storage closet.

Marcus had learned to measure success differently during the eighteen months of construction and program development—not in architectural awards or profit margins, but in the number of children who had safe places to go after school, adults who had found employment through job training programs, elderly residents who received daily meals and social interaction that kept them connected to community life. The statistics were impressive, but the stories were what mattered most: families who had avoided eviction through emergency assistance, teenagers who had stayed in school because of tutoring support, adults who had discovered new careers because someone believed they were worth investing in despite their age or previous setbacks.

The sound of voices in the fellowship hall interrupted his solitary reflection—the choir arriving early for final rehearsal before the service, voices that had learned to harmonize not just in music but in the daily work of creating sanctuary for people who needed safe spaces to practice healing together. Angela Martinez had become more than choir director; she was program coordinator for the arts initiative that provided creative outlets for children and adults who had discovered that broken people could still make beautiful music if they had opportunities to practice restoration in community with others who understood the relationship between beauty and survival.

"Marcus, we're ready for sound check," Angela called from the doorway, her voice carrying the confidence of someone who had found her calling in work that aligned her musical gifts with her passion for community development. The young woman who had arrived at Mount Zion three years earlier as a grief-stricken daughter caring for a dying father had become a leader whose influence extended far beyond Sunday morning worship to encompass programming that served the entire community.

The sound system was one of many technological upgrades that had been necessary to transform a traditional church into a multiuse community facility—hearing assistance devices for elderly participants, projection equipment for job training presentations, recording capability for oral history projects that preserved the stories of people whose experiences might otherwise be lost when their generation passed away. The equipment was expensive but essential, enabling programming that required professional-quality audiovisual support rather than the makeshift arrangements that had characterized previous community events.

Marcus followed Angela into the sanctuary and took his place at the piano, an instrument that had been donated by a foundation board member who had been moved by the testimonies she heard during Mount Zion's site visit. The piano was beautiful and functional, capable of accompanying everything from traditional hymns to contemporary music that reflected the diverse tastes of community members who ranged in age from preschoolers to centenarians.

But it was the voices that transformed musical instruments into something approaching transcendence—forty-three people who had learned to blend individual gifts into collective expression that was stronger and more beautiful than any single voice could produce alone. The choir included congregation members who had been singing at Mount Zion for decades alongside community members who had never been inside a church before discovering that musical participation was possible without religious commitment, that artistic expression could serve spiritual purposes even for people whose relationship with organized religion was complicated by personal or political considerations.

They began with "Precious Lord," the hymn that had sustained Ruth Washington through her own struggles with grief and disappointment, that had become Marcus's touchstone during the months when grant applications were rejected and construction problems threatened to derail the renovation project entirely. But today the arrangement was different—less about individual petition and more about collective celebration, less about asking for divine intervention and more about offering thanks for grace that had already been received through the patient work of human hands guided by divine vision.

The harmony was complex but natural, voices that had learned to trust each other through months of rehearsal and community building, through the shared experience of creating something beautiful from whatever gifts each person could contribute regardless of formal training or previous musical experience. Mrs. Patterson's granddaughter sang soprano despite being only twelve years old, her clear voice rising above the adult harmonies with the confidence of someone who had never been told that children should be heard from but not listened to.

James Wilson's bass anchored the lower harmonies, his voice carrying the weight of someone who had found employment through the job training program and wanted to give back to the community that had invested in his potential when he was fifty-eight years old and had thought his working life was over. The construction skills he had learned through Mount Zion's programs had enabled him to find steady work with contractors who needed experienced workers willing to learn new techniques and safety protocols.

As the rehearsal continued, Marcus found himself thinking about the distance between the young civil rights activist his mother had been and the community development worker he was becoming, between the dramatic confrontations that had characterized the movement of Ruth's generation and the patient institution-building that seemed to define social justice work in his own era. The lunch counter protests and voter registration drives had been necessary and heroic, but they had also been episodes that began and ended, victories that could be celebrated and defeats that could be mourned within defined timeframes.

Community development work was different—less dramatic but more sustainable, focused on creating systems that could serve people's daily needs rather than winning symbolic victories that might not translate into improved living conditions for families dealing with poverty and educational disadvantage and the accumulated effects of decades of systematic disinvestment in communities that had been deemed economically unviable by policy makers who had never lived with the consequences of their decisions.

The transformation of Mount Zion had required skills that Marcus was still developing—not just architectural expertise, but grant writing and volunteer coordination, conflict resolution and program evaluation, the ability to work collaboratively with people who possessed different expertise and different perspectives on how to solve problems that affected everyone but that no one could address through individual effort alone.

But it had also required something that Ruth had spent her entire life teaching him—faith that individual gifts were meant to serve collective needs, that community problems could be solved through sustained effort and creative partnership, that some work was worth doing regardless of its impact on personal advancement or professional recognition.

The rehearsal ended with "Amazing Grace," arranged in the traditional call-and-response pattern that had sustained African American churches through slavery and segregation and now this peculiar form of economic exile that left communities intact but emptied of the structures that had once provided purpose and direction for people's daily lives. But the song felt less like lament and more like testimony, less about being lost and more about being found, less about individual salvation and more about collective transformation that had happened through the patient work of people who had refused to let destruction have the final word in conversations about what was possible when faith and works joined hands in service of something larger than anyone could achieve alone.

As the choir members dispersed to prepare for the service, Marcus remained at the piano, running his fingers across keys that had been blessed by countless hours of practice and performance, by music that had provided comfort during grief and celebration during joy, by voices that had learned to harmonize despite differences in age and experience and theological perspective that might have divided them if they had focused on disagreement rather than discovering common ground in shared commitment to community well-being.

The dedication service would officially mark Mount Zion's transformation from struggling congregation to thriving community resource center, but Marcus understood that the real dedication had happened through eighteen months of daily choices to prioritize service over comfort, collaboration over control, long-term impact over immediate gratification. Every grant application had been an act of faith, every construction decision had required trust in outcomes that could not be guaranteed, every program launch had demanded belief that people would participate in services that had never existed before and might not succeed despite good intentions and adequate funding.

The challenges had been substantial and ongoing—contractors who didn't understand the difference between commercial renovation and community development, foundation program officers who needed constant updates on progress that often felt too slow to measure, congregation members who sometimes struggled with changes that disrupted familiar routines even when the changes served important purposes. Marcus had learned to navigate conflicts between preservation and adaptation, between honoring tradition and serving contemporary needs, between maintaining Mount Zion's identity as a house of worship and expanding its function as a community resource center.

But the results spoke for themselves in ways that architectural awards or professional recognition never could—children who had safe places to go after school, adults who had found employment through job training programs, elderly residents who received daily meals and social interaction, families who had access to social services that helped them navigate crises without losing their homes or their hope for better circumstances.

David joined him at the piano, settling onto the bench with the careful movements of a seventy-four-year-old man whose arthritis had been acting up during the humid summer weather. His father looked older than he had eighteen months earlier, but also more purposeful, energized by involvement in work that honored Ruth's memory through practical service rather than sentimental tribute.

"Your mama would be amazed," David said, his words carrying the weight of someone who had known Ruth well enough to speak with confidence about her probable response to the transformation that surrounded them. "Not surprised—she always believed this kind of thing was possible—but amazed that it actually happened, that enough people caught the vision to make it real."

Marcus nodded, understanding that Ruth's amazement would be less about architectural achievement than about community collaboration, less about professional success than about the evidence that individual gifts could serve collective flourishing when people decided that some things were more important than personal advancement or individual recognition.

The conversation was interrupted by the arrival of Keisha Daniels, who entered the sanctuary carrying flowers and the particular combination of excitement and exhaustion that characterized her approach to events that she had been planning for weeks but that still required last-minute attention to details that could make the difference between meaningful celebration and chaotic disappointment.

"The reporter from the Durham Herald is here," she announced, referring to the journalist who would be documenting Mount Zion's dedication service for a feature story about innovative approaches to community development in rural Southern towns.

"She wants to interview you before the service starts, get some background about how the project came together."

The media attention was gratifying but also intimidating—external validation of work that had felt uncertain for months, professional recognition that could help other congregations pursue similar projects, but also pressure to articulate lessons learned and best practices that could be replicated in different contexts with different resources and different community needs.

Marcus had been reluctant to position himself as an expert in community development work that he was still learning through trial and error, through mistakes that had taught him as much as successes about the complex relationship between architectural renovation and social programming, between physical space and community building, between individual leadership and collective ownership of projects that required sustained commitment from people who would be using services and programs long after the renovation was completed.

"Tell her I'll talk to her after the service," Marcus said, preferring to let the dedication ceremony speak for itself before attempting to explain lessons that he was still processing, insights that were still forming as he learned to measure success differently than his corporate architectural practice had taught him to evaluate professional achievement.

The sanctuary began filling an hour before the service was scheduled to begin, people arriving early to tour the renovated facilities and reconnect with neighbors they might not have seen since the previous community event. The crowd was more diverse than traditional Mount Zion services—not just in terms of age and race, but in terms of relationship to organized religion, including people who participated in community programming but had never attended worship services, who valued the social services and cultural activities that Mount Zion provided without necessarily sharing the theological convictions that had motivated the congregation's expansion into community development work.

The diversity felt like success to Marcus—evidence that Mount Zion had become what Ruth Washington had been individually, a source of practical help and spiritual encouragement for anyone who needed either or both, regardless of their formal religious affiliation or their ability to contribute financially to the programs they were receiving. The community center model had attracted foundation funding precisely because it served broader purposes than traditional church programming, because it addressed genuine social needs through sustainable services rather than limiting ministry to people who shared specific doctrinal commitments.

But the diversity also created challenges that Marcus was still learning to navigate—how to maintain Mount Zion's identity as a Christian congregation while serving people whose spiritual needs were met through different traditions or whose relationship with organized religion had been damaged by experiences that made church attendance feel unsafe or unwelcome. The balance between evangelism and service, between sharing faith and respecting difference, between maintaining congregational identity and embracing community diversity required constant attention and frequent recalibration as programs evolved and participant needs became clearer.

Mother Caldwell arrived in a wheelchair pushed by her great-niece, her one-hundred-year-old body too frail for independent mobility but her mind still sharp enough to serve as keeper of institutional memory and dispenser of wisdom that came from witnessing Mount Zion's entire history from construction through multiple reconstructions to this latest transformation. She had insisted on attending the dedication service despite her declining health, understanding that her presence would provide continuity between Mount Zion's founding generation and whatever future awaited the community resource center that bore the same name but served purposes that the original builders could never have imagined.

"Help me to the front pew," she instructed her great-niece, her voice carrying the authority of someone who had earned the right to special accommodation through decades of faithful service and community leadership. "I want to see everything, want to remember this day when I'm too old to remember much of anything else."

The comment carried poignancy that was not lost on congregation members who understood that Mother Caldwell represented the last living link to Mount Zion's earliest years, that her death would mark the end of firsthand memory about the vision and sacrifice that had created the foundation on which all subsequent ministry had been built. Her presence at the dedication service felt like blessing and commissioning combined—approval from the generation that had built Mount Zion originally, encouragement for the generation that was responsible for ensuring its survival and continued relevance in a community whose needs had evolved dramatically since the 1950s.

The service began with a processional that included not just the pastor and choir, but representatives from every program that Mount Zion now housed—the after-school coordinator and her student assistants, the job training instructor and recent graduates who had found employment through skills they had learned in the renovated basement, the nutrition program coordinator and elderly participants who had found not just meals but fellowship that kept them connected to community life despite mobility limitations and transportation challenges.

The processional felt less like religious ceremony and more like community celebration, acknowledgment that Mount Zion's transformation had been accomplished through collaborative effort rather than individual achievement, through the contributions of people who possessed different skills and resources but who shared commitment to creating something that could serve others rather than just themselves.

Pastor Williams delivered the invocation, but his prayer acknowledged the presence of people who might not share his theological convictions while affirming values that transcended denominational boundaries—commitment to human dignity, dedication to community well-being, faith in the possibility that people working together could solve problems that individuals could not address alone. The prayer was Christian in its language but universal in its vision, inclusive enough to embrace participants who valued Mount Zion's community programming without necessarily embracing the religious framework that had motivated its expansion.

The scripture reading came from Isaiah 61, the passage about bringing good news to the poor and binding up the brokenhearted, about proclaiming liberty to captives and setting prisoners free, about comforting those who mourn and providing for those who grieve. But Pastor Williams applied the ancient words to contemporary circumstances—the economic captivity that trapped families in cycles of poverty, the grief that accompanied loss of employment and educational opportunity, the need for liberation from systems that limited human potential based on zip code and family income rather than individual gifts and community support.

It was exactly the kind of biblical interpretation that had sustained the civil rights movement—the understanding that sacred texts spoke to contemporary circumstances, that ancient promises could guide modern action, that individual faith was incomplete without practical commitment to collective justice. But it was also interpretation that acknowledged the complexity of social problems that could not be solved through dramatic confrontations or symbolic victories, that required the patient work of institution building and service delivery and the kind of daily attention to human needs that sustained communities through gradual change rather than revolutionary transformation.

The dedication began with Marcus presenting the ceremonial key to Mother Caldwell, recognizing her as the representative of Mount Zion's founding generation and the person whose approval mattered most to congregation members who had risked everything on the vision of transformation that surrounded them. The key was symbolic rather than functional—the building had electronic locks and security systems that had been required by insurance companies and funding organizations—but the gesture acknowledged continuity between past and future, between the faith that had built Mount Zion originally and the faith that had sustained its renovation and expansion.

Mother Caldwell accepted the key with hands that trembled but held firmly, her grip reflecting determination that had outlasted every challenge Mount Zion had faced during her century of life. "This key represents more than access to a building," she said, her voice amplified by the new sound system but carrying strength that technology could not provide. "It represents access to hope, to opportunity, to the kind of community that treats every person as if they carry God's image within them."

She paused, gathering breath and strength for words that would be remembered long after the dedication service was concluded, that would be quoted in newspaper articles and foundation reports and the oral history project that was documenting Mount Zion's transformation for future generations who would need to understand how vision became reality through sustained effort and collaborative faith.

"I have lived long enough to see this church destroyed twice by people who thought they could stop our faith by burning our building," she continued, her words carrying across the sanctuary with the authority of personal witness to Mount Zion's entire history. "I have lived long enough to see it rebuilt twice by people who understood that our sanctuary was not made of wood and brick but of the love that brought us together to serve each other."

The silence that followed was thick with recognition that they were witnessing something unprecedented—not just the dedication of renovated facilities, but the testimony of someone who had lived through Mount Zion's complete story, who could speak from personal experience about the persistence required to outlast destruction, the faith necessary to rebuild from ashes, the vision needed to transform crisis into opportunity.

"Today I am living long enough to see it transformed into something that serves more people than ever before, that provides more hope than we ever imagined possible when we laid the first foundation stones seventy years ago. This building is not just our church anymore—it is our community's church, our neighborhood's church, our city's church. And that is exactly what it was always meant to be."

The applause that followed was not just appreciation but celebration, recognition that Mother Caldwell had articulated what many people felt but had struggled to express—that Mount Zion's transformation represented more than architectural renovation, more than program expansion, more than successful fundraising. It represented proof that communities could adapt and survive and thrive when people decided that some things were worth preserving through change rather than protecting from change, worth expanding rather than contracting, worth sharing rather than hoarding.

The testimonies that followed illustrated the practical impact of Mount Zion's transformation through stories that statistics could not capture, human experiences that demonstrated why community development work mattered more than professional recognition or financial profit. Angela Martinez spoke about discovering that grief could be transformed into music that helped other people heal, that individual pain could serve collective restoration when it was offered in community with others who understood the relationship between suffering and service.

James Wilson described finding employment at age fifty-eight through job training programs that had prepared him not just with technical skills but with confidence that he still had valuable contributions to make despite economic changes that had eliminated the manufacturing jobs he had expected to support his family through retirement. The construction work he had found through Mount Zion's programs paid decent wages and provided health insurance that had seemed impossible to obtain as an unemployed middle-aged worker with limited formal education but extensive practical experience.

A teenage girl named Destiny spoke about the after-school program that had provided homework assistance and college preparation support that her single mother could not afford but that had made the difference between high school graduation and dropout, between college acceptance and minimum-wage employment that would have perpetuated cycles of poverty that had limited her family's opportunities for generations.

Each testimony reinforced the same theme—that individual transformation happened in community contexts, that personal success required institutional support, that private struggles could be addressed through public commitment to creating systems that served human flourishing rather than just economic efficiency.

But the testimonies also revealed the ongoing challenges that Mount Zion's programs were addressing—unemployment and underemployment that forced people to choose between rent payments and medical care, educational disadvantage that limited children's opportunities despite their intelligence and motivation, isolation and depression that affected elderly residents who had outlived many of their peers and struggled to maintain social connections that made life worth living.

The problems were substantial and persistent, rooted in economic and political systems that operated according to priorities that often conflicted with community well-being and individual dignity. Mount Zion's programs could not solve systemic issues, but they could provide support and resources that helped people navigate difficult circumstances with greater success and less desperation, that offered hope and practical assistance to families who might otherwise fall through social safety nets that were designed more to manage poverty than eliminate it.

As the testimonies concluded and the service moved toward its formal dedication, Marcus found himself thinking about Ruth Washington and what she would make of the transformation that surrounded them—not just the physical renovation that had created beautiful and functional space, but the programmatic expansion that had made Mount Zion a source of daily support for hundreds of people who needed what it offered.

Ruth had spent her career teaching children to believe in their own potential despite circumstances that argued against hope, helping families navigate educational and economic systems that were designed to serve people who already had advantages rather than people who needed opportunities to develop their gifts and contribute their talents to community well-being. Her work had been personal and individual, focused on one student at a time, one family at a time, one relationship at a time.

Mount Zion's community center model was different in scale but identical in spirit—institutional commitment to the same values Ruth had practiced individually, systematic application of the same principles she had embodied personally, organizational expression of the same faith she had demonstrated daily through choices that prioritized service over comfort, other people's needs over her own convenience.

The dedication prayer was offered by Pastor Williams, but it included voices from throughout the congregation and community—people who had participated in the renovation project, who had benefited from expanded programming, who had contributed skills and resources and hope that had made transformation possible. The prayer was less petition than thanksgiving, less request for divine blessing than recognition of grace that had already been received through human collaboration guided by shared vision and sustained by stubborn faith.

As the prayer concluded and the congregation began to move toward the fellowship hall for the meal that followed all Mount Zion celebrations, Marcus remained in the sanctuary for a few minutes, alone with the silence that held everything—the prayers and struggles and hopes that had filled this space for seventy years, the dreams and disappointments that had tested and strengthened faith in equal measure, the accumulated wisdom of people who had learned to build something beautiful from whatever materials were available when conventional resources proved inadequate.

The silence felt different now—less empty and more full, less waiting and more anticipating, less questioning and more affirming. It was the silence of sanctuary that had been achieved rather than sanctuary that was still being sought, the silence of work that was being completed rather than work that was still being imagined, the silence of community that had been built rather than community that was still being hoped for.

The silence was speaking, and what it said was this: that love was stronger than fear, hope more durable than disappointment, community more powerful than any force that sought to divide and diminish the human capacity for building something beautiful together. The silence held all of it—the prayers offered in desperation and the prayers offered in gratitude, the dreams deferred and the dreams fulfilled, the faith that had sustained three generations of Mount Zion members through every form of destruction that hatred and indifference could devise.

But it was also the silence of new beginnings rather than final endings, of possibilities that were being opened rather than chapters that were being closed. The transformation of Mount Zion from struggling congregation to thriving community resource center was not the end of its story but the beginning of a new chapter that would be written by children who were learning to read in after-school programs, adults who were developing job skills in basement workshops, elderly residents who were finding fellowship around tables where they shared meals and memories and hopes for grandchildren who would inherit whatever world the adults managed to build or preserve.

Angela's voice reached him from the fellowship hall, calling the community choir to lead the blessing for the meal that would be served to anyone who wanted to stay, regardless of their formal connection to Mount Zion or their ability to contribute to the cost. The song she had chosen was "Blessed Assurance," arranged in harmony that reflected the diversity of voices that now called Mount Zion home—not just congregation members but community members, not just people who shared theological convictions but people who shared commitment to each other's well-being, not just those who had always belonged but those who had found belonging through programs and services and the simple recognition that everyone deserved to be treated as if they carried divine spark within them.

Marcus joined the singing as he walked toward the fellowship hall, his voice blending with others in music that expressed what words alone could not capture—gratitude for grace received, commitment to work that remained, hope for community that was still being built one relationship at a time, one program at a time, one act of service at a time.

The meal was served cafeteria-style by volunteers who included congregation members and program participants, foundation board members who had driven from Raleigh to attend the dedication service, local officials who wanted to understand how Mount Zion's model might be replicated in other communities facing similar challenges. The diversity of the serving line reflected the diversity of the community that Mount Zion now served—not just people who looked alike or thought alike or worshipped alike, but people who had decided that some things mattered more than differences, that human dignity transcended denominational boundaries, that community well-being required collaboration across lines that often divided people who should have been working together.

The conversations around the dinner tables touched on practical concerns and visionary possibilities—how to sustain programming that depended on grant funding, how to maintain building systems that were more complex than traditional church facilities required, how to balance congregational identity with community service, how to measure success in work that addressed problems that could never be completely solved but that could be addressed with patience and creativity and the kind of sustained effort that produced gradual improvement rather than dramatic transformation.

But the conversations also revealed the satisfaction that came from participating in work that aligned individual gifts with collective needs, that served purposes larger than personal advancement or professional recognition. The foundation program officer who had initially approved Mount Zion's grant application spoke about how rare it was to find projects that delivered on their promises, that actually served the populations they claimed to serve, that demonstrated measurable impact without losing sight of human dignity and community empowerment.

The contractor who had supervised the renovation described learning about community development work through hands-on experience with projects that required different approaches than commercial construction, that prioritized community participation over efficiency, that valued local hiring and skills development as much as technical competence and deadline compliance.

A grandmother whose grandchildren participated in the after-school program talked about how different their lives had become since they had safe places to go when school ended, adults who believed in their potential despite academic struggles, programming that addressed their individual needs rather than treating them as problems to be managed or statistics to be processed.

Each conversation reinforced the same themes that had emerged throughout the dedication service—that individual transformation happened in community contexts, that sustainable change required institutional support, that some problems could only be addressed through collaborative effort that brought together people with different skills and resources but shared commitment to outcomes that served everyone's interests rather than just immediate participants.

As the afternoon wore on and the crowd began to thin, Marcus found himself in conversation with the reporter from the Durham

Herald, answering questions about the renovation project and Mount Zion's model for community development.

"What would you say to other architects who might be interested in community development work?" she asked, recognizing that Marcus's career transition might inspire other professionals to consider applying their skills to social problems.

"That it requires learning new skills and unlearning old assumptions," Marcus replied. "The technical challenges are often simpler than commercial projects, but the human challenges are much more complex. Success is measured differently—not in architectural awards or profit margins, but in whether the building actually serves the community needs that justified its renovation."

The reporter leaned forward, interested. "Do you miss the financial rewards and professional recognition from your Atlanta practice?"

"I make less money but sleep better at night," he said, understanding that the comment would probably appear in the newspaper article but feeling confident that it accurately represented his experience. "The financial sacrifice has been significant, but the personal satisfaction has been even more significant. This is the first time in my career that I've felt like my professional expertise was directly serving the community that invested in my education."

As the interview concluded and the reporter departed, Marcus began gathering his things. David joined him near the fellowship hall entrance, already being prepared for the evening's programming.

"Long day," David said, settling into a folding chair with the exhaustion that came from events that were emotionally as well as physically demanding.

"Good day," Marcus replied, understanding that his father was acknowledging the completion of work that had honored Ruth's memory through practical service rather than sentimental tribute, that had transformed grief into action and loss into legacy that would serve future generations of people who would benefit from programming and services that existed because a community had decided that some things were worth building regardless of the risks that building required.

The conversation was interrupted by voices from the sanctuary—the community choir gathering for evening rehearsal, people who had discovered that individual voices could combine to create harmony that was stronger and more beautiful than any single person could produce alone. Angela was leading them through a new arrangement of "Amazing Grace," setting parts that accommodated the range of vocal abilities represented in a choir that welcomed anyone who wanted to participate regardless of formal training or previous musical experience.

"Want to join them?" David asked.

Marcus nodded. As they walked toward the sanctuary, the voices grew louder, blending in harmonies that were still finding their shape—harmonies that would continue the ongoing work of creating beloved community one relationship at a time, one program at a time, one act of faithful service at a time.

In the sanctuary, voices joined in harmony that rose toward heaven like prayers made audible, like hopes given sound, like love transformed into music that could be heard and felt and shared by anyone who needed to know that they were not alone, that community was possible, that silence could speak when it held the accumulated prayers and dreams and stubborn faith of people who refused to let destruction have the final word in conversations about what could be built when individual gifts were offered in service of collective flourishing.

Marcus took his place at the piano as the choir found their positions, voices that had learned to trust each other through months of practicing harmony that required individual gifts to serve collective beauty. The song they began was one Ruth had loved—"Blessed Assurance"—but tonight it sounded different, seasoned by the day's celebration and weighted with understanding of what assurance actually meant when it was lived rather than simply sung.

The melody began with Angela's clear soprano, joined by Mrs. Patterson's granddaughter whose twelve-year-old voice carried the confidence of someone who had never been told that children should be heard from but not listened to. James Wilson's bass anchored the lower harmonies, his voice reflecting the satisfaction of a man who had found employment and purpose through programs that had invested in his potential when the broader economy had written him off as too old and too displaced to matter.

But it was the harmony itself that told the real story—individual voices blending into something that was stronger and more beautiful than any single person could create alone, differences in age and experience and formal training becoming assets rather than obstacles when everyone was committed to creating beauty together rather than competing for individual recognition.

Marcus felt his fingers find the familiar chord progressions, muscle memory guiding him through accompaniment that supported without overwhelming, that provided foundation without demanding attention. This was what he had learned in eighteen months of community development work—that leadership was often about creating space for other people's gifts to flourish, about offering expertise in service of collective vision rather than using expertise to demonstrate personal importance.

The second verse brought additional voices as people from the evening programs joined the choir, adults from the literacy class and the support group adding their voices to music that welcomed participation regardless of formal training or religious affiliation. A teenager from the after-school program began improvising harmony that showed musical gifts no one had known she possessed until Mount Zion provided opportunities for discovery and development.

This was what Ruth would have celebrated most—not the architectural achievement or the successful fundraising, but the evidence that people were finding their voices, discovering their gifts, contributing to collective beauty in ways that individual talent could never achieve alone. The community center model had succeeded not just in providing services but in creating space where human potential could unfold in directions that surprised even the people who possessed gifts they had never been encouraged to develop.

The song built through verses that acknowledged struggle while insisting on hope, that named disappointment while choosing faith, that recognized the reality of problems while refusing to let problems define the limits of possibility. By the final verse, the choir had grown to include nearly forty voices—congregation members and community participants, people who had been singing together for years and people who had never sung in public before tonight.

As the last notes faded into silence that was full rather than empty, Marcus felt something he had been reaching toward his entire adult life without quite being able to name—the deep satisfaction that came from using individual gifts in direct service of collective flourishing, from applying professional expertise to problems that affected people he cared about rather than clients who simply needed technical services.

The choir members began to disperse toward their various evening commitments—homework help for children whose parents were working second jobs, support group meetings for families dealing with addiction, literacy classes for adults who needed basic skills to qualify for job training programs. But their voices lingered in the sanctuary's acoustic space, harmonies that seemed to resonate in the wooden beams and stained glass windows that had absorbed decades of music, prayer, and stubborn faith.

Angela approached the piano as Marcus gathered his music, her face carrying the particular combination of exhaustion and exhilaration that characterized people who had found their calling in work that challenged them professionally while serving purposes they could support personally.

"Thank you," she said simply, but her words carried weight that went beyond gratitude for piano accompaniment to acknowledgment of collaboration that had made tonight's celebration possible, recognition of leadership that had created space for her own gifts to serve community needs rather than just personal expression.

"Thank you for everything you've brought to this place," Marcus replied, understanding that Angela's transformation from grief-stricken daughter to community choir director and program coordinator exemplified what Mount Zion's ministry was actually accomplishing—not just providing services but creating opportunities for people to discover that their own gifts could serve purposes larger than individual need or private satisfaction.

The conversation was interrupted by laughter from the fellowship hall, where the support group was concluding its meeting with the kind of shared joy that happened when people discovered they were not alone with struggles that had seemed impossible to bear in isolation. The after-school program was wrapping up with a reading circle where children practiced skills that would help them succeed academically while adults provided attention and encouragement that busy parents couldn't always offer after long days of work that barely covered basic expenses.

This was what success looked like in community development work—not dramatic transformations or breakthrough moments, but the accumulation of small improvements in daily life that helped people navigate difficult circumstances with greater hope and more practical support. Children who had safe places to go after school, adults who learned job skills that could lead to stable employment, elderly residents who shared meals and friendship that kept them connected to community life despite mobility challenges and health problems.

The statistics were impressive—Mount Zion now served more than three hundred people monthly through programming that addressed everything from child care to job training to social services—but the numbers could not capture what mattered most: the quality of attention that people received, the dignity with which they were treated, the respect that was shown for gifts and potential that other institutions often overlooked or undervalued.

Marcus locked the piano and began turning off lights in the sanctuary that would be quiet until morning, when the cycle would begin again with breakfast for elderly residents who lived alone, followed by job training workshops for adults seeking employment, then after-school programming for children whose academic success required more support than their families could provide independently.

The routine had become familiar over eighteen months of operation, but it still felt remarkable to Marcus that this level of programming was happening in a building that had been on the verge of closure, that was being sustained by a congregation of forty-three mostly elderly members supplemented by community volunteers and professional staff whose salaries were covered by grants and donations from people who believed in Mount Zion's mission even if they had never set foot in the building.

David was waiting in the fellowship hall, having spent the evening moving between different programs as unofficial host and informal supervisor, providing the kind of grandfatherly presence that helped people feel welcome regardless of their formal connection to Mount Zion or their comfort level with church-based programming.

"Ready to head home?" David asked, though home was now the same house where they had been processing Ruth's death when the insurance crisis had forced decisions about Mount Zion's future, where architectural drawings had been spread across the kitchen table next to boxes of Ruth's papers that documented a lifetime of service to individual students and community needs.

The house felt different now—less like refuge from challenging work and more like preparation for challenging work, less like escape from community responsibility and more like restoration for community leadership that required energy and patience and the kind of sustained commitment that could only be maintained through regular renewal of spirit and purpose.

At home, the kitchen table that had served as mission control for Mount Zion's fundraising campaign was now covered with materials for the next challenge—proposals and correspondence from other congregations interested in what Mount Zion had accomplished, each one representing communities facing similar struggles to transform crisis into sustainable mission.

"You know," David said, settling into his chair with coffee that had become their evening ritual for processing the day's experiences and planning the next day's priorities, "your mama always said that the most important work was the work that had to be done again every day, that didn't stay done once you finished it."

Marcus nodded, understanding the difference between construction projects that ended and community development work that required ongoing attention.

"Teaching was like that for her," David continued, his words carrying the weight of forty-five years of marriage to someone whose professional satisfaction came from work that was never finished, that required starting over with new students each year, new challenges each day, new opportunities to invest in human potential that could not be guaranteed to produce the results she hoped for but that was worth pursuing regardless of outcomes she could not control.

"She used to say that the best work was work that made other work possible—that taught people to solve their own problems, that created systems that could serve needs even when she wasn't there to provide individual attention. Sounds like that's what Mount Zion is doing now."

"I keep thinking about something Mother Caldwell said during the dedication," Marcus said, referring to the afternoon's ceremony that now felt like weeks ago despite having concluded only hours earlier. "About this building being our community's church now, not just our congregation's church. I think that's what Mama was trying to teach me my whole life—that individual gifts don't really belong to individuals, that they belong to the communities that make them possible."

David smiled with the recognition of someone who had watched Ruth practice that philosophy daily through career choices that prioritized service over salary, through volunteer commitments that served community needs rather than enhancing her own reputation, through the patient work of treating every person as if they carried divine potential that deserved investment and encouragement regardless of external circumstances.

"She would be proud of what you've built here," David said, gesturing toward the materials on the table that represented ongoing work rather than completed achievement, future challenges rather than past victories. "But she'd also want to make sure you understood that you didn't build it alone, that it exists because a lot of people decided to use their gifts in service of something bigger than any one person could accomplish independently."

The reminder was gentle but important—that community development work succeeded through collaborative leadership rather than individual heroics David smiled with the recognition of someone who had watched Ruth practice that philosophy daily through career choices that prioritized service over salary, through volunteer commitments that served community needs rather than enhancing her own reputation, through the patient work of treating every person as if they carried divine potential that deserved investment and encouragement regardless of external circumstances.

"She would be proud of what you've built here," David said, gesturing toward the materials on the table that represented ongoing work rather than completed achievement, future challenges rather than past victories. "But she'd also want to make sure you understood that you didn't build it alone, that it exists because a lot of people decided to use their gifts in service of something bigger than any one person could accomplish independently."

The reminder was gentle but important—that community development work succeeded through collaborative leadership rather than individual heroics, through the coordination of diverse skills

Marcus gathered the materials from the table and prepared to end the long day that had begun with dedication ceremony and concluded with choir rehearsal, that had included media interviews and community meals, testimonies and celebration that marked Mount Zion's transformation while pointing toward work that remained to be done. Tomorrow would bring routine programming and administrative responsibilities, grant reports and partnership meetings, the daily discipline of maintaining community services that had become essential to families who depended on them for child care, job training, social support, and the sense of belonging that came from participating in community life that welcomed their contributions rather than just tolerating their presence.

Upstairs in his childhood bedroom that now served as home office for community development work, Marcus looked out the window toward Mount Zion's building where security lights illuminated the sign that identified it as both Baptist church and community resource center. The building stood solid and purposeful in the darkness, its renovated facilities ready for tomorrow's programming. In the distance, a freight train called its lonesome song toward destinations unknown, but Mount Zion's lights remained steady, marking a place where people had decided that some things were worth preserving through change rather than protecting from changes done. Tomorrow would bring routine programming and administrative responsibilities, grant reports and partnership meetings, the daily discipline of maintaining community services that had become essential to families who depended on them for child care, job training, social support, and the sense of belonging that came from participating in community life that welcomed their contributions rather than just tolerating their presence.

The dedication was complete, but the building continued—the ongoing work of creating beloved community one relationship at a time, one program at a time, one act of faithful service at a time. When the silence spoke, what it said was this: that some things endured not because they were protected from destruction but because they were rooted in love that was stronger than fear, hope that was more durable than disappointment, community that was more powerful than any force that sought to divide people who had learned that they belonged together in the patient work of building something beautiful from whatever materials grace provided and stubborn faith made possible.